"Are you going somewhere?" Jackson asked.

"Home."

"It might be best if you stay in the hospital," he said.

"That's what the doctor keeps telling me, but I'm feeling well enough to leave."

"It's not just your physical condition I'm worried about, Morgan. The men who attacked you are still loose. Until they're found, the hospital is the safest place."

"They've got no reason to come looking for me again."

"They didn't get what they wanted, did they?"

"No."

"That's more than enough reason."

Morgan sighed. "Look, I'm grateful for everything you did tonight, but I really am fine."

"And I can go back to wherever I came from? Sorry, I don't work that way," Jackson said.

"What way *do* you work, then?"

"I stick with what I start. I started protecting you from two men who wanted you dead. I'm not going to walk away until I'm sure I've achieved that goal."

Books by Shirlee McCoy

Love Inspired Suspense

Die Before Nightfall
Even in the Darkness
When Silence Falls
Little Girl Lost
Valley of Shadows
Stranger in the Shadows
Missing Persons
Lakeview Protector
The Guardian's Mission
The Protector's Promise
Cold Case Murder
The Defender's Duty
**Running for Cover*

*The Sinclair Brothers
**Heroes for Hire

Steeple Hill Trade

Still Waters

SHIRLEE McCOY

has always loved making up stories. As a child, she daydreamed elaborate tales in which she was the heroine—gutsy, strong and invincible. Though she soon grew out of her superhero fantasies, her love for storytelling never diminished. She knew early that she wanted to write inspirational fiction, and began writing her first novel when she was a teenager. Still, it wasn't until her third son was born that she truly began pursuing her dream of being published. Three years later she sold her first book. Now a busy mother of five, Shirlee is a homeschool mom by day and an inspirational author by night. She and her husband and children live in Washington and share their house with a dog, two cats and a bird. You can visit her Web site at www.shirleemccoy.com, or e-mail her at shirlee@shirleemccoy.com.

Shirlee McCoy

RUNNING *for* COVER

Steeple
Hill®

Published by Steeple Hill Books™

STEEPLE HILL BOOKS

Steeple
Hill®

Recycling programs
for this product may
not exist in your area.

ISBN-13: 978-0-373-44384-0

RUNNING FOR COVER

www.SteepleHill.com

Printed in U.S.A.

I led them with cords of human kindness,
with ties of love; I lifted the yoke from their
neck and bent down to feed them.

—Hosea 11:4

To my fifth treasure, Qian Annalise—
I am not your first mother or even your second,
but I will be your last. It is true that you were not
born from my body, but you have always lived in
my heart—first a thought, then a prayer and now a
reality that fills me up to overflowing.

You are mine, my cheeky girl, and I am yours.
Forever and a day, to the edges of the universe and
beyond, I love you.

ONE

Pain.

It pulled Morgan Alexandria from silky blackness, slammed her into reality. She groaned, levering away from cold tile, crimson blood dripping from her lips and staining the white kitchen floor. More blood pooled in her mouth, the metallic taste of it making her gag. She wanted to sink back down, let whatever was going to happen happen. Images flashed through her mind—blond hair, deep blue eyes, chubby cheeks; dark hair and a solemn, thin face. Morgan's sister and brother as they'd been twenty years ago.

What were they like now?

The question drove Morgan to her knees. She blinked, trying to clear her vision and her head. Sounds were coming from the den. Soft thuds and thumps. Rumbling voices. Morgan could wait for the two armed men who'd come into her gallery an hour ago to return to the kitchen or she could run. Either way, she'd probably die.

She staggered to her feet, her jaw and head throbbing in time with her racing heart. Just a few yards and she'd be at the door of the apartment. One flight of stairs down and she'd be in the small gallery she'd opened nearly a year ago when she'd foolishly believed she could cut her ex-husband Cody out of her life forever. She should have known that the trouble and heartache he'd brought to their marriage would follow her.

A loud crash startled her into action, and she ran, broken glass from the upended coffee table crunching under her feet as she raced through the living room. Her fingers brushed the doorknob, her hand closing around cool metal.

Almost free.

Hard fingers dug into her shoulder, yanking her away from the door and escape.

"You don't get to leave until we get the disk. Just tell us where it is, and you can walk out of here." The voice was as hard as the grip on her shoulder, and Morgan knew it was full of lies. There'd be no leaving. Just a slow, painful death or a quick, brutal one. Terror gave her strength, and she swung around, slamming her fist into the man's eye.

He cursed, his grip loosening, and Morgan wrenched her shoulder from his grasp, grabbing the doorknob again and yanking the door open. She took the stairs two at time. Praying. Begging. Hoping God heard.

The gallery at the bottom of the stairs was dark, the room silent. No evidence of the violence that had taken place there in the minutes before Morgan had been dragged up to her apartment.

If she died, how long would it take for anyone to notice she was gone?

Her footsteps echoed through the large room as she raced for the front door, her heart pounding harshly in her ears. Just a few more feet. Just a few more seconds.

Please, please, please. I'm not ready to die.

The prayer caught in her throat, a barely formed scream dying as she was jerked backward. Her sweater tightened around her throat and stars danced in front of her eyes, darkness beckoning again. It would be so easy to give up. To give in. But there were too many things left undone, too many words left unsaid.

Too many regrets.

She clawed at the fabric of the sweater, fighting for air.

"Cool it. You kill her and we'll never get what we came for," a man said.

And suddenly Morgan could breathe again.

She collapsed onto the floor, coughing and gagging as one of the men leaned down, stared into her face. "You shouldn't have punched me. We could have made this easy on you. Now…well, maybe it won't be so easy after all. Come on. Get up. We're going back upstairs and you're going to tell us what you did with the disk."

"I already told you I don't have it," Morgan managed to say, the words as dry and brittle as old bones.

"That's not what your ex-husband said." The man grinned, the hot, ugly look in his eyes making Morgan wish she could sink back into unconsciousness.

"Whatever Cody told you—"

The chime of the doorbell interrupted her, and Morgan froze, her gaze jumping to the gallery door. The sound came again, soft but insistent.

"You expecting a visitor?" Her captor hissed the words as he pressed a gun to her temple.

Morgan nodded, lying. Praying it would save her. Praying that the person on the other side of the door was someone she knew. Someone who would see the fear in her eyes, the bruises on her face and go for help.

"Whoever it is, get rid of him. If you don't, his blood is on your hands." He dragged her to her feet, motioned for the other man to step into the deep shadows of the gallery and then shoved Morgan to the door.

Her hands shook as she cracked it open just enough to see a man standing on the front stoop. Tall and rangy, his face shadowed by darkness, he was a stranger.

Morgan's heart sank. "Yes?"

"I saw a light on and thought you might be open."

"No. I'm sorry, we're not." Morgan forced the response past lips that felt swollen and tight. She wanted to shove the door open and run, but knew she'd be shot before she took half a dozen steps. And she wasn't the only one who'd die.

"Too bad. I saw the closed sign, but hoped since your lights were on you might be willing to make a sale. A friend of mine is getting married in the morning, and I just realized I left his wedding gift at home in New York." Despite the darkness, Morgan could see his easy, charming smile. He didn't know how close he was to death, and Morgan didn't dare try to tell him.

"I wish I could help you, but I've got a wedding to attend tomorrow, too. I've got a lot to do before then, so if you'll excuse me…"

"Really?" He smiled again. "Maybe it's the same one."

"What?"

"Wedding. Who are the bride and groom?" He shifted as he spoke, easing a little to the left, his gaze focused on a point above Morgan's head. Could he see the man standing deep in the shadows? Or the one right beside Morgan hidden behind the door? Did he sense the danger they were both in?

The hard butt of a gun jammed into Morgan's side, urging her to answer the question and get rid of her visitor. For a moment she couldn't remember what the question was, couldn't think of what the answer would be.

The man at the door took a step forward, his gaze still on the point above Morgan's head. And everything clicked into place. The question. The answer. "Lacey Carmichael and Jude Sinclair are the bride and groom."

"It *is* the same wedding. I guess we'll see each other there."

The gun jabbed into Morgan's side again, a silent warning

she couldn't ignore. "I guess we will." If she lived that long. "Now I really have to go."

"Sure. No problem. What time to do you open in the morning?"

Open? What time *did* she open?

Morgan's mind was blank, her thoughts scattered.

"Ma'am?"

"Ten. I open at ten."

"I'll see you then," he said, turning to walk away.

No. You won't. I'll be dead, sprawled on the floor of my apartment or wrapped in a plastic bag on the side of a road or lying on the bottom of the lake, cement blocks tied to my ankles.

Morgan wanted to shout the words, wanted to beg for rescue. Instead, she closed the door, her skin crawling as she met the eyes of the man who'd been standing next to her. Mud-brown, they were empty of emotion.

"Good job. That guy has you to thank for his life," he said, shoving his gun into a holster beneath his jacket.

"Come on. We've wasted enough time. Let's finish this," the second man said from the shadows, his voice gravelly and rough. "Let's go back upstairs and get what we came for."

Morgan didn't see him move, but she heard his booted feet on the stairs. Knew he was going back to her apartment.

"Let's go. Maybe a little more convincing will help you remember where you put the disk." The other man grabbed her arm, forced her toward the stairs.

"I told you, the disk isn't here," she protested, tugging against his hold.

"Like I said, that's not what your ex said."

"Cody is a liar."

"Even a liar tells the truth when he's in enough pain."

"Pain? He's in jail." Morgan twisted beneath his grip, hoping to dislodge his fingers, but they dug deep into her flesh until she was sure her bone would break. A few more feet and they'd reach the stairs.

Desperate, she grabbed a clay vase she'd fired just a few days ago, slamming it into her captor's head. He fell back, and Morgan broke away, racing to the door and yanking it open. Cool air stung her bruised face as she closed the door and jumped off the stoop, crashing into something yielding but firm. She tried to scream, but a hand clamped over her mouth, cutting off the sound. Morgan fought, kicking and punching as an arm wrapped around her waist and pulled her tight against a hard chest.

"Calm down, lady. I don't know what's going on here, but I'm not in the mood for trouble, so until I figure things out, let's both lie low." The gruff baritone seemed familiar, but Morgan was too scared to care. She twisted and pulled against his arm as he maneuvered her into the heavy bushes that hugged the foundation of the gallery.

"Someone's coming. You need to keep still and quiet. Understand?" the man whispered, his lips pressed close to Morgan's ear.

She nodded, but wasn't sure she understood anything. Not how a peaceful night at home had turned into a nightmare or how her jailed ex-husband could still be ruining her life or who the man holding her was.

"Good, because Jude won't be happy if I'm a no-show tomorrow." His grip eased, his hand slipping away from Morgan's mouth, his other arm still wrapped tightly around her waist.

Footsteps sounded on pavement, the quick, hard tap of booted feet sending a shiver along Morgan's spine and filling her with terror. Hiding wasn't good enough. They needed to run. She shifted, but was held firmly in place as the footsteps faded. The loamy scent of earth filled her nose, mixing with something subtle and masculine. Morgan should be terrified, should be fighting to free herself and run, but her head throbbed, her ribs ached and the warmth of the man holding her, the darkness that surrounded them, offered a false sense of safety that she wanted desperately to believe in.

The man who held her leaned close to her ear again, his breath ruffling her hair as he spoke. "Who is he? Boyfriend? Husband?"

"No."

"A stranger?"

"Yes. Two of them. They've got guns," she rasped out, the words too loud and harsh.

"Stay here, I'll—"

"No." Morgan grabbed his arm. She didn't know anything about him, but right now having him around was a lot better than being alone.

"We can't sit here waiting to be found."

"Maybe they'll go away."

"No, they won't. Stay down. I'm just going to look and see what direction they're heading." He eased away, moving so silently Morgan heard nothing but the rapid pulse of her blood and the rasping gasp of her breath.

She waited a few seconds, her heart slamming against her ribs. At any moment one of the men who'd held her captive in her own home, who'd beaten her unconscious and left her lying bleeding on the kitchen floor, could find her and it would all be over. All the hard work she'd put into opening her gallery, Clay Treasures, all the years she'd spent dreaming of reuniting with her siblings, all the time she'd spent searching for them, would end on the pavement of a parking lot in a small town she never would have come to if not for her ex-husband. Trusting Cody, letting him into her heart had been the biggest mistake of Morgan's life. She'd vowed after her divorce to rely only on herself, yet here she was, sitting in the darkness, waiting for someone else to save her life.

The air seemed heavy with tension, the night thick with expectancy. Morgan eased up from her hiding place, peeked over the top of the shrubs and saw nothing but darkness. Fear spurring her on, she broke free of the prickly shrubs and ran to the corner of the building. For one brief exhilarating moment, she was sure she'd succeed. That somehow she'd escape the parking lot and make it out onto the street without being seen. There were neighbors who would let her in and call the police for her. All she had to do was make it to one of their doors.

Behind her, someone shouted, the sound breaking through the silence. Morgan dodged to the right, screaming as wood siding splintered inches from her face.

"Get down!"

The words barely registered as Morgan was tackled from behind. She landed hard, the breath leaving her lungs in a quick, painful rush.

"Are you crazy, lady? I told you to stay down!" He rolled away, and Morgan stayed put, barely able to breathe, much less move. She turned her head, trying to see what was happening, and saw her would-be rescuer pull something from beneath his jacket.

A gun! He had a gun!

He aimed at something behind him, fired and grabbed Morgan's hand, pulling her up and into a dead run before she had time to realize she was moving. Something exploded inches from her feet, bits of asphalt flying up and hitting her calf. She screamed again and again, her throat raw from it.

"Come on. Faster!" The man beside her nearly yanked her off her feet as he sprinted into the street.

Morgan's lungs burned, her legs shaking as he pulled her up the stairs and to the front door of the nearest house. He banged on the wood, his fists pounding hard enough to shake the door.

Morgan wanted to tell him that the woman who lived inside was eighty-five, hard of hearing and unlikely to open the door even if she heard him banging, but the words wouldn't form. Darkness edged in, blurring her vision and stealing her thoughts. She swayed, knew she was falling but couldn't seem to right herself.

"Whoa! No passing out. I can't hold you and fire a gun at the same time."

The grumbled command was the last thing Morgan heard as she fell into oblivion.

TWO

Jackson Sharo pulled the unconscious woman up against his chest, shielding her from the street as best he could. Gun in hand, he shifted his stance, glancing over his shoulder, the hair on the back of his neck standing on end. He'd come to Lakeview, Virginia, for his friend's wedding. He hadn't come for trouble. Unfortunately, trouble had found him.

He scowled, kicking the door.

"Open up. I've got an injured woman out here. We need help," he shouted, wishing he still had the right to call himself a police officer. That was a lot more likely to get a door opened than kicking it and shouting would.

A light in the house went on and a shadow passed in front of the window to the left of the door.

"I've called the police. They'll be here any minute," a shaky voice called out.

"Call an ambulance, too. And open the door. We need help," Jackson responded, tensing as a car passed by on the street behind him. A bullet in the back wasn't the way he planned to end the night.

The woman he was holding stirred, pushing against his chest, her soft hair brushing Jackson's chin as she raised her head and mumbled something he couldn't hear.

"What?" he asked, looking down into her face. A dark bruise covered her left jaw. Another marred her cheek. Blood seeped from her forehead and shadowy marks on her neck hinted at other injuries. If he hadn't shown up, she'd be dead by now. The thought made him cold with rage. He'd seen injuries like hers one too many times during his years as a New York City homicide detective, had experienced firsthand the devastation of losing a loved one to violence. No way would he let it happen to someone else.

"I said that her name is Mrs. Richardson. Tell her Morgan needs her help. She'll open the door," she repeated as she tried again to lever away from Jackson's chest.

"Mrs. Richardson? I've got Morgan out here with me. She's hurt."

A face pressed against the window, and Morgan twisted in Jackson's grip, offering a quick wave that seemed to reassure the elderly woman.

The door opened, and she hovered in the threshold, white hair puffed around a powder-pink face that nearly matched the color of her flowered bathrobe. "Morgan?"

"I'm afraid so," Morgan said, her voice shaky.

"Come on. Inside." Jackson kept his hold on her waist and urged her into the house, not waiting for further introductions or an invitation.

"What in the world happened to you?" Mrs. Richardson put a hand on Morgan's arm, her gaze darting to Jackson and to the gun he held, her eyes widening with fear.

"Some men came into the gallery right before I closed. They—"

"I'm going to look for them," Jackson cut in. "Close and lock the door when I leave. Don't let anyone but the police inside." There were two armed men on the loose and no time for chitchat.

"You can't. They could kill you." Morgan grabbed his arm,

her grip surprisingly strong. Her bruises looked darker in the stark fluorescent light, her eyes pale silvery-blue, the pupils dilated. Trembling with fear or with shock, she didn't look capable of staying on her feet, let alone arguing with Jackson. Somehow, though, she was managing it.

"The police should be here soon." Jackson pulled off his jacket, draping it around her shoulders, hoping to warm her.

"But—"

He didn't let her finish, just walked outside, pulling the door closed, his gun still firmly in hand. The sense of danger and urgency he'd felt while waiting for Mrs. Richardson to open her door had dissipated, and Jackson jogged back to the gallery, knowing the men were already gone, the opportunity to bring them into custody gone with them.

Except for his car, the parking lot was empty, light from the upstairs windows spilling onto the pavement. The gallery's double doors yawned open, inviting Jackson to explore the darkened area beyond. If he hadn't spent nine years as a police officer, he might have, but he knew that contaminating the evidence would make prosecuting a lot more difficult.

He turned away from the building, searching the area for any signs of the men who'd been there. There was nothing. No bullets. No casings. No tread marks, cigarette butts or trash. Everything clean and tidy and free of clues.

Jackson had just completed a circuit of the area when a squad car raced into the parking lot, lights and sirens off. An officer jumped out, her frantic energy freezing Jackson in place. No way did he want to get shot by a police officer, and the way the cop pulled her gun and pointed it in his direction, getting shot looked like a distinct possibility.

"Drop the weapon, sir, and step away from it," she ordered.

Now wasn't the time to explain things, so Jackson did as she asked.

She eased forward, lifting the gun, her gaze never wavering. "Facedown on the ground, sir. Hands where I can see them."

Jackson knew the drill. He'd issued the same command enough times in his years on the New York City police force. He dropped to the ground, waiting impatiently as the officer checked the safety on his gun, frisked him for weapons and pulled the wallet from his pocket.

"I guess you have a permit for your gun?" Judging from the way she asked the question, Jackson figured she didn't guess any such thing.

"I do. I'm a private investigator. My ID and permit are in my wallet."

The deputy opened the wallet and took her time looking through it. Finally, she seemed satisfied with what she'd found. "You can get up, Mr. Sharo. Did you fire your weapon tonight?"

"One shot."

"Did you hit your target?"

"Unfortunately, no," he said as he accepted the wallet she held out to him.

"I'm not sure the law would agree with that."

"I was firing in self-defense, Officer…?"

"Deputy Lowry. Want to tell me what happened here?"

"I saw a light on in the gallery and thought it might be open for business. When I rang the doorbell a woman answered. She looked beat-up and scared, so I searched the perimeter of the building to try to get a feel for what was going on."

"You didn't think to call the police?"

"For all I knew, she'd been in an accident of some sort and didn't need help."

"So, you walked around the house and…?"

"I didn't see any reason to be concerned." But he hadn't been able to shake the feeling that something was wrong or to forget the look of stark terror in Morgan's eyes. "I was going to leave, but decided to check on the owner one more time. Before I got to the door, she ran out. Next thing I knew, two men were shooting at us."

"And you fired back."

"One shot." He repeated the answer he'd given before, knowing he'd probably be asked the same thing a hundred times before the night was over.

"Have you been back in the gallery since you fired the shot?"

"I was never in the gallery."

"I see."

Before she could explain what she thought she saw, another squad car pulled into the parking lot. The door opened and a tall, dark-haired man got out. He wasn't alone. Morgan sat in the passenger seat, huddled beneath a blanket, a coffee mug cupped in her hands. She met Jackson's gaze, offering a smile that turned into a grimace of pain.

"You should be on your way to the hospital," he said as he walked to the vehicle, ignoring the deputy's sputtered protest.

"She will be," the man offered before Morgan could reply. "I've already called an ambulance, but Morgan wanted to make sure you were all right while we waited for it. I'm Sheriff Jake Reed."

"Jackson Sharo."

"From New York?" The sheriff's brow furrowed and he cocked his head to the side, studying Jackson.

"That's right."

"You're here for the Sinclair wedding?"

"Right again."

"Jude told me you were coming. Said you were partners when you worked homicide in New York. I'm surprised you're not hanging out with him. This being his last night as a bachelor and all."

"That's exactly what I'd be doing if I hadn't run into trouble."

"I guess what I'm asking is how you ended up at Morgan's gallery tonight."

"I'm happy to tell you, but you might want to get some men out looking for the perps before you waste time listening to my story."

"I've already taken Morgan's statement and issued an APB based on her description of the suspects. Doesn't mean I don't want to hear your story." If the sheriff was annoyed by Jackson's comment, his tone and expression didn't show it.

"You want the long or short version?"

"Either will work."

"I was working on a case and missed my flight out of New York last night. I wasn't sure I'd be able to get another flight, so I drove down here. I got into town a few hours ago and realized I'd left Jude and Lacey's gift in New York. After Jude's rehearsal dinner, I decided to drive around town to see if I could find a place to buy one."

"So that's the short version?"

"Yeah." The long version was something Jackson didn't plan to share. He had wanted to find a gift for his friend, but he'd also needed space. Seeing Jude's family together had reminded Jackson of his own family and the loss that had torn them apart. It was that more than anything that had driven him to his solitary search for a gift. If he'd been the kind to believe that God intervened in the business of men, Jackson would be tempted to think that He'd put him in just the right place at just the right time to save Morgan's life.

"Tell me what happened when you got here," the sheriff said, interrupting Jackson's thoughts.

Jackson gave him as many details as he could, his gaze drawn to the squad car and the woman inside it. She looked vulnerable, her eyes hollow and empty. Jackson had gone into police work to help people like her. He'd left it because he'd failed when it counted most. The truth was a hard knot in his chest. He cleared his throat, wishing he could clear his mind of the past as easily. "That's as much as I know. I think the rest of your answers will have to come from Morgan."

"All right. Thanks. Are you staying with Jude?"

"Yes."

"Leaving after the wedding tomorrow?"

"I'd planned to do some fishing and head back to New York Sunday morning."

"Then I'll let you get back to what you were doing, but I'll want to ask a few more questions before you leave town. How about we meet after the wedding reception?"

"Sure." Not that he had a choice in the matter.

"You have a business card?"

"In my wallet. Your deputy still has it."

"Here you go, Mr. Sharo." She dropped it into Jackson's outstretched palm.

"And my gun?"

The sheriff nodded, and the deputy returned that to Jackson, as well. That meant he could do exactly what the sheriff had suggested and get back to the wedding gift hunt.

It was probably what he should do. It was even what he wanted to do, but Jackson knew he couldn't. Quitting the police force hadn't changed his desire to serve and protect. As much as he wanted to, he couldn't leave until he was sure Morgan would be all right. "You said you called an ambulance?"

"Should be here in a few minutes."

"A few minutes or an hour, it doesn't matter, because I'm not going to the hospital," Morgan said as she eased out of the squad car, leaving the blanket and coffee cup behind.

"I think we discussed this already," the sheriff said. "You need to be checked out at the hospital. We've got a victim's advocate there who will talk to you and help you through the process." His tone was implacable, but Morgan didn't seem to notice.

"I'm not a victim." Despite the argumentative tone, her voice trembled, and Jackson wondered how long it would be before her tough facade crumbled and she crumbled with it.

"Sheriff Reed is right. You need to let the doctors take a look at your injuries." He put a hand on her shoulder, letting it fall away when she flinched.

"I don't need a doctor to tell me I've been beaten. And I don't need a victim's advocate to tell me it wasn't my fault."

"Then what do you need?"

Jackson's question must have surprised her. She met his gaze, her almond-shaped eyes surrounded by thick black lashes that contrasted sharply with light-colored irises. "To go back a decade and say no when my ex-husband asked me to marry him."

"You think your ex-husband had something to do with what happened tonight?"

"*Something* to do with it? He had everything to do with it. The men who were here were searching for something of Cody's. A disk. They said Cody told them that I had it. That he'd given it to me before he went to prison."

Her ex-husband was in prison?

And she owned an art gallery in Lakeview, Virginia.

And her first name was Morgan.

Surprised, Jackson studied her face. Bruised and swollen, it barely resembled the photo of Morgan Alexandria that he'd seen months ago when Jude Sinclair had asked him to investigate the ex-wife of a man he'd put into prison. Barely resembled but did. Dark black hair. Vivid, silvery-blue eyes. Exotic beauty that had stuck in his mind long after he'd seen the photo. Maybe if he hadn't been so caught up in escaping his thoughts and his guilt, Jackson would have put two and two together when he'd first arrived at the gallery.

And maybe he wouldn't have rung the doorbell.

Seen Morgan's battered face.

A God thing?

His sister would have said so.

Maybe, just maybe, Jackson believed it.

An ambulance pulled into the parking lot, cutting off further conversation.

"Looks like your ride is here, Morgan," the sheriff said quietly. "I'm going to check things out around here. Then I'll come by to see how you're doing."

"Really, Sheriff Reed, I don't need to go to the hospital. All I need are a few aspirins and an ice pack."

Of course, she *did* need to go. There'd be a team waiting to collect forensic evidence from her clothes, hair and skin. Photographs would be taken. Doctor's reports written. Everything done to ensure that anything collected would be admissible in court.

Sheriff Reed didn't mention any of those things as two EMTs approached. Jackson didn't either, but the thought of Morgan facing doctors, police and victim's advocate alone didn't sit well with him.

"Is there anyone you want me to call for you, Morgan? Family? Friends? Someone who can meet you at the hospital?"

"No. Thanks."

An EMT dropped a blanket over her shoulders and urged her toward the ambulance. She took a few steps and stopped, turning to face Jackson. "In case I don't see you again, thanks. For everything. If you hadn't shown up—" she paused, shaking her head. "Thanks."

In case I don't see you again.

The words were eerily similar to the ones Jackson's sister had spoken two and a half years ago. They'd been at their parents' house, celebrating their youngest sister's engagement.

At the end of the evening, Lindsey had hugged Jackson tight, kissed his cheek and told him she loved him. Surprised, he'd laughed and asked what all the mushy stuff was about. Her words had haunted him ever since, echoing in his mind and drifting into his dreams. *I just want you to know how I feel. In case something happens and we never see each other again.*

She'd followed the remark with a quick comment about Jackson's dangerous line of work, and they'd parted ways. A month later, Lindsey was dead, murdered by her estranged husband. Too late, Jackson heard her words for what they were—a cry for help. He couldn't go back and change the past, couldn't redo that moment, ask the questions that should have been asked. What he *could* do was make sure that Morgan really was okay.

An hour at the hospital, and Jackson would get back to what he'd come to Lakeview for. Tomorrow, he'd watch as Jude and Lacey vowed to love each other forever, he'd pray that their forever was much longer than his sister's had been, and then he'd row out onto Smith Mountain Lake, inhale the cool autumn air and hope that somehow he'd find the peace he'd been searching for since Lindsey's death.

THREE

Morgan pulled on a borrowed sweatshirt, wincing as the fabric brushed against her bandaged forehead. She'd told Sheriff Reed that all she needed were a few aspirins and an ice pack and she'd be fine. That was before the pain hit. Now she thought she might need a couple days in bed and some heavy-duty painkillers before she felt better. Her head throbbed, her jaw ached and her ribs hurt with every breath. Though the doctor assured her nothing was broken, moving was painful, and Morgan grimaced as she shoved her feet into sneakers that were a size too big and leaned down to tie the laces. At least she had shoes. The clothes she'd been wearing during the attack had been taken as evidence. If not for the kindness of several nurses, Morgan would be stuck wearing a hospital gown home.

And she *was* going home.

Despite the doctor's recommendation that she stay for twenty-four-hour observation, Morgan was determined to return to the gallery as soon as Sheriff Reed gave her the okay. She had calls to make and packing to do. It had been two years since she'd last visited her family in Spokane, Washington. She'd thought there would be plenty of time for trips west after she established her gallery, but no one was guaranteed a tomorrow. Thanks to Cody and his thug friends, Morgan realized that now more than ever.

"Ms. Alexandria?" A young nurse poked her head into the room, her wide-eyed gaze making Morgan feel like a bug under a microscope. Worse, it made her feel like a victim, and that was something she'd promised herself she'd never be again.

"Yes?"

"There's someone here to see you."

"I'd rather not—"

Before she could get the words out, a man nudged past the nurse and stepped into the room. Morgan recognized him immediately. Rangy and tall with auburn hair and midnight-blue eyes, he looked exactly like a hero should—tough, trustworthy and strong.

Or maybe the fact that he'd saved Morgan's life was skewing her perspective. "Jackson? What are you doing here?"

"Making sure you're all right." He said it as if coming to the hospital to visit a stranger was the most natural thing in the world. And they *were* strangers despite the way Morgan's heart leaped in recognition as she looking into his eyes.

"Shouldn't you be out searching for a wedding present for Jude and Lacey instead?"

"That can wait," he said, his gaze dropping to the too-large shoes she wore. "Are you going somewhere?"

"Home."

"It might be best if you stay here for the night."

"That's what the doctor keeps telling me, but I'm feeling well enough to leave."

"It's not just your physical condition I'm worried about, Morgan. The two men who attacked you are still on the loose. Until they're found, the hospital is the safest place for you."

"If they want to find me, the hospital is going to be no safer than anyplace else."

"If?" he asked, raising an eyebrow, the gesture as practiced as the charming smile he'd flashed when she'd opened the gallery door. He reminded her of Cody. The same easy charm and playboy exterior that hid more than it showed. She glanced away, uncomfortable with the comparison and with her own need to make it.

"They've got no reason to come looking for me again."

"They didn't get what they wanted, did they?"

"No."

"That's more than enough reason. They risked a lot tonight. I doubt they'll back down now. You said they wanted a disk that your husband gave you, right?"

"My *ex*-husband. And he didn't give me anything." The last gift he'd given her had been the diamond-and-ruby heart pendant he'd presented to Morgan on their sixth anniversary. It had been too expensive and ostentatious to wear, and after the divorce Morgan hadn't felt at all bad about selling it and all the other jewelry he'd given her to help finance her gallery.

"Maybe it's packed away in a box somewhere. Is it possible he slipped it into your belongings without you knowing it?"

"No offense, Jackson, but I've been asked these questions at least a dozen times by three different deputies. I'd rather not answer them again until Sheriff Reed gets here."

Morgan eased down into a chair by the window. She wanted out of the hospital and out of the mess she'd suddenly found herself in. A mess of Cody's making.

Of course.

That seemed to have been the pattern of their lives while they were married. Cody messing up. Morgan cleaning up.

"You okay?" Jackson asked, crossing the room and crouching down in front of Morgan, his hand touching hers for just a moment, the warmth of it remaining after he let it fall away.

"Fine. I'm just ready to get out of here. I've got things to do before tomorrow."

"You look pale. How about I call the nurse?" He leaned

closer, his eyes deep blue and flecked with gold and deep brown. An interesting color. The kind a woman could get lost in if she let herself.

Morgan wouldn't let herself. She'd been down that path before, been interested, attracted and then in love. All she'd gotten from that was trouble. "Look, I appreciate your concern, and I'm grateful for everything you did tonight, but I really am fine."

"And I can go back to wherever I came from?"

"Something like that."

"Sorry, I don't work that way," he said, straightening, stretching. He was tall with a lean, hard build. More runner than bodybuilder, but he had a presence that made him seem larger than life.

"What way do you work, then?"

"I stick with what I start. I started protecting you from two men who wanted you dead. I'm not going to walk away until I'm sure I've achieved that goal."

"You can't be serious." Appalled, Morgan stood, trying not to wince as the throbbing in her head and jaw increased. The last thing she needed was a man like Jackson hanging around trying to play hero. She'd worked too hard to become independent, she'd struggled too long to convince herself that going it alone was better than working as a team. There was no way she was going to allow herself to depend on someone, to *believe* in someone again.

"Sure I can," he said, dropping a hand onto her shoulder, offering her support she didn't want to need. "Why don't you sit down before you fall down?"

"Why don't you—"

A soft knock sounded on the door, and a pretty blonde stepped into the room, cutting off Morgan's words. "Morgan! Thank goodness, you're all right."

"Lacey, what are you doing here?" Surprised, Morgan allowed herself to be pulled into a quick hug. Slender and lovely, Lacey Carmichael had proven to be a good friend during the months since they'd met. Morgan was cautiously excited about her friend's engagement to Jude Sinclair and hopeful that Lacey would have a lot more happiness in her marriage than she'd had with Cody.

"Jude called to let me know you were in the hospital. I insisted he pick me up before he came here. He's parking the car, but he'll be here in a minute."

"Are you both nuts? You're getting married in a few hours. You should be home sleeping, dreaming of that happily-ever-after you've always wanted."

"While you were here alone? Neither of us could do that."

"I'm not alone," Morgan said, shooting a glance in Jackson's direction. He smiled, obviously amused by her attempt to use him despite her insistence that he leave.

"And you won't be. Are you okay? Have they found the men who did this to you?"

"No, but it's over, and I'm all right. That's what matters."

"And we're going to make sure you stay that way. Jude and I discussed it on the way here. We're going to postpone our honeymoon until the men who attacked you are caught."

"There is no way I'm going to let you stay here babysitting me."

"Your well-being is more important than a trip to Paris," Jude Sinclair said as he walked into the room. Tall and lean, he'd come to Virginia to recover from a nearly fatal attack. When he'd showed up at Morgan's gallery asking questions about her ex-husband, she'd recognized him immediately as the homicide detective who'd put Cody in jail.

To say it had taken a while for them to become friends was putting it mildly. Morgan was thrilled that Lacey had found someone to love, but being around Jude still put her on the defensive.

She forced herself to relax and to meet his probing gaze. "I appreciate the concern, Jude, but I'm old enough to take care of myself."

"That's not the point, Morgan, and you know it," Lacey cut in. "This is about friendship. I can't go to Paris and enjoy myself knowing that someone I care about is in danger."

"Who said I was in danger? For all we know, tonight was a one-time thing." Morgan lied deftly, not liking the taste of it on her tongue, but unwilling to let Lacey give up a honeymoon trip to Paris to keep her safe.

Nothing could keep her safe.

Nothing but running, and that was one thing Morgan excelled at. She'd been running for more years than she cared to admit. No sense in giving that up now.

"The fact is, I'm not sticking around. After your wedding tomorrow, I'm taking off."

"To where?"

"Does Jake know this?"

Lacey and Jude spoke in unison, and Morgan decided to answer the first question and ignore the second. "Washington."

"D.C.?"

"State. It's where I grew up."

"I thought you were from New York," Jude said, eyeing Morgan with suspicion.

"I moved there after I married Cody." She didn't offer more of an explanation.

"We were housemates for months and you never mentioned Washington." Lacey sounded more hurt than suspicious and the throbbing in Morgan's head increased. Guilt was something she didn't need any more of, but somehow she always managed to find it.

"I haven't been back there in years. Now seems like a good time to visit."

"Do you really think you can outrun the guys who came after

you tonight?" Jackson asked. He'd moved a few feet away, but still seemed to take up more than his fair share of space.

"That's not why I'm leaving. I have some…loose ends to tie up in Washington. Some family I need to reconnect with."

"I'll go with you," Lacey said, her green eyes filled with worry and anxiety. She should be happy and excited about her wedding the following day. Not worrying about Morgan.

And guilt clawed another path up Morgan's throat. She felt sick with it. Or maybe she was sick from the pain in her head and in her jaw. "I'm ruining what should be the most fantastic time in your life. I'm sorry."

"I'm marrying the man of my dreams. There's nothing that can ruin that."

"There's no need for anything to be ruined," Jackson cut in. "I'm here. I'll make sure that Morgan stays safe until the police figure out what's going on or until you two get back from Paris. Whichever comes first."

"You can get the time off?" Jude asked, frowning slightly.

"I'll work it out."

"You don't need to work anything out," Morgan responded, trying to regain control of the situation, but neither man seemed to hear.

"You're sure?"

"Absolutely." Jackson smiled, his gaze on Morgan. She was sure he was trying to convey something with his unwavering stare, but for the life of her, Morgan couldn't figure out what it was.

"You two can discuss this all you want, but I don't need or want Jackson sticking around," she said, and Jackson responded with a brief shake of his head.

Obviously, he *was* trying to tell her something.

"*You* don't, but if it'll ease our friends' minds to know that I'm here looking out for you, what'll it hurt for me to stick around?"

And she *finally* got it.

He had no intention of playing bodyguard. He simply wanted to reassure Jude and Lacey so they could enjoy their wedding and honeymoon. *That* she could do. *That* she could deal with. "All right. If it'll help everyone feel more comfortable, I'll agree to it."

"You will?" Lacey sounded so shocked, Morgan would have smiled if she hadn't been in so much pain.

"Every once in a while, I see the sense in someone else's plan. Jackson has a good one. You and Jude will have a wonderful day tomorrow and a wonderful week away, and I'll be perfectly fine while you're gone." Fine *without* Jackson, but Morgan didn't say that.

"Oh, Morgan, thank you!" Lacey pulled Morgan into a gentle hug.

"Don't thank me. Thank Jackson. It was his plan." His lie. But Morgan didn't say that, either. She had too many of her own issues. Too much of her own sin to deal with. No way did she plan to point fingers at someone else until she could look in the mirror and stop seeing all the mistakes she'd made.

"Thank you, too, Jackson," Lacey said "You don't know how much this means to me."

"Sure I do." Jackson smiled and accepted Lacey's hug, his gaze meeting Morgan's again.

"I hate to interrupt the love fest, but I just finished at the crime scene, and I need to get some information from Morgan," Jake Reed said as he strode into the room, a small notebook in his hand. He looked grim and unhappy, his jaw set and his lips drawn into a thin, hard line. Bad news had a look to it. A hardness and ugliness that no amount of trying could hide. Jake had that look, and Morgan braced herself to hear whatever he had to say.

"What is it? Did you find something?"

"Nothing significant. We've got a couple of smudged prints, the tread of a shoe in the blood on your kitchen floor. We'll see if it matches to your shoe."

"What else?"

"Nothing. The guys who attacked you were thorough. Professional. They didn't leave hair or clothes fibers. We're checking on some blood in the gallery. It may belong to one of our perps."

"Okay." Morgan took a deep breath. Waiting. Waiting. There was more. She was sure of it.

"While the forensic evidence team worked, I made some phone calls. Thought it wouldn't be a bad idea to check up on your ex."

"And?"

"I've got some news that you may not want to hear, but it's got to be said."

"So just say it."

"Cody Bradshaw is dead. He was killed by an inmate three days ago."

"He's dead?" Morgan couldn't wrap her mind around the thought. Vibrant, larger than life Cody. Dead.

The words didn't seem to go together.

"I'm afraid so."

"Why wasn't I told?"

"His parents were listed as next of kin. Since you and Bradshaw are divorced, you weren't contacted. I guess your in-laws didn't bother to let you know?"

"No." They wouldn't have. They still blamed her for their son's incarceration. According to the Bradshaws, Morgan had led their son down a path to destruction. They'd cut ties with her before the divorce was final.

She'd been happy to let them.

It was the way she'd wanted it. No contact with Cody. No contact with his parents. No contact with the past.

Too bad the past refused to let her go.

"Are you okay?" Jackson's hand rested on her shoulder, his fingers warm through her borrowed T-shirt. Morgan wanted to tell him that she was fine. That hearing of Cody's death wasn't nearly as hard as hearing that he'd murdered his business partner had been. But the words stuck in her throat, and all she could do was nod.

"I've got a call into the warden. Hopefully by tomorrow we'll have more information about what happened. Until then, I want to offer my sincere condolences," Jake said, his grim expression never easing.

"Thank you."

"Morgan, I'm so sorry." Lacey's eyes were filled with tears, and Morgan wanted to tell her to save them for something more tearworthy, but she knew how harsh that would sound. How wrong.

The fact was, she'd loved Cody once. Might have continued to love him if he hadn't betrayed her one too many times. In the nearly two years since he'd been in prison, Morgan hadn't wasted time missing him and had rarely spent time thinking about him. But that didn't mean she wanted him dead.

"It's okay. I'm okay," she offered, fighting tears she wouldn't shed. There'd be a time to mourn the loss of life, but it wasn't now. It wasn't here. Later, when she was walking through the vivid green pasture behind her parents' house, when she was staring up at the deep blue foothills of the Rocky Mountains, when she was all alone except for the grass and the sky and God, then she would cry. For Cody. For herself. For what they could have had, but had never managed to create.

"Can you think of anyone who would want your husband dead, Morgan?" Sheriff Reed asked.

"Ex-husband," she said by rote. As if it mattered any longer.

"Sorry. Your ex. Is there anyone you can think of who had a grudge against him?"

"Not offhand. Cody could be charming when he wanted to be."

"Did he always want to be?"

"If you're asking if he had enemies, then you'll have to ask someone else. Cody kept his business life separate from our life together." He'd kept other things separate, too, but Morgan decided not to say as much. Not now with a roomful of people listening.

"If you think of anything…"

"I'll let you know. Is there anything else you needed to ask? Because I'm exhausted, and I'd really like to go home."

"Nothing that can't wait for another time. I've got a cleaning crew getting your apartment and gallery in order. You may want to stay here for the night."

"I'd rather not."

"You can stay with me," Lacey offered, but Morgan shook her head.

"I need to pack."

"Pack?" Jake speared her with a hard gaze.

"I need to put some distance between myself and what happened tonight. I thought I'd go stay with my parents for a while."

"And they're where?"

"Washington."

"That's a long way from here."

"I know."

"Tell you what, write down what town you're going to be in. Give me your parents' address. I'll call the local police and make sure they're aware of what's going on. They can keep an eye out on things on their end while I investigate here."

"I appreciate it, Sheriff Reed."

He eyed her for a moment and then nodded, handing her his notebook and a pen. "Write the information down for me. Then you can be on your way."

She did as he asked, her hand shaking as she scribbled her parents' address, her mind racing with memories. The day she'd met Cody. The day she'd brought him home to meet her parents. The soft, sweet scent of summer rain as they'd fished in the pond behind her parents' house. The quiet joy of finally feeling accepted and loved.

The disappointment of knowing it was all a lie. The sweet words and tender touches. The whispered promises and deep, meaningful gazes. The vow to love forever.

Lies.

And now Cody was dead and it was too late to do it over. To try it again. To hope for something better.

A tear dropped onto the pad of paper, and Morgan brushed it away angrily.

"Are you sure you don't want to stay with me, Morgan?" Lacey asked, and Morgan glanced up, saw that four pairs of eyes were watching her intently.

"I'm sure," she said, forcing a smile as she handed the pad back to the sheriff. "But I wouldn't mind a ride home if someone can give me one."

"I'll drop you off," Sheriff Reed offered. "That way I can make sure you're locked in tight before I leave you alone."

"You don't have to worry about that. I'm going to lock and bolt every door."

"I'll call you when I get home, okay?" Lacey said, her green eyes shadowed with worry as she and Jude walked to the door.

"We'll talk tomorrow. At your reception. Or have you forgotten that you're getting married in ten hours?"

"Twelve, but who's counting?" Lacey smiled, some of the worry easing from her face.

"You. Now go home and get some sleep or everyone in Lakeview will blame me for the dark circles under your eyes tomorrow."

"Be careful, okay?"

"I will." Morgan offered a quick wave as Lacey stepped out of the room.

"You're sure you want to go home?" Jake shoved the small notebook into his back pocket, and Morgan nodded.

"Yes."

"All right. Let's get out of here, then. You coming, Sharo?"

"I'm heading back to Jude's place," Jackson replied, following as Sheriff Reed led Morgan from the room.

Morgan could feel the heavy weight of his gaze as they made their way down the hall to the nurse's station and then outside into the crisp fall night. Jackson was an attractive man. A very attractive one. He was also a liar. Morgan had watched him in action, heard the sincerity in his words as he'd offered to keep her safe.

A handsome, charming liar.

Just like Cody.

So why was she almost sorry to see him go when he climbed into his sporty black car and drove away?

"Because you're an idiot. That's why," she muttered as she slid into Jake's police cruiser.

"You say something?" he asked.

"Nothing important."

He nodded and closed the door, leaving Morgan in silence as he rounded the car and got in. She wanted to break the quietness as they drove toward her house, but could think of nothing to say. There were too many thoughts and too many memories, none worth the effort it would take to put them into words.

She'd fallen in love with Cody. She'd married him. He'd broken her heart. Now he was dead.

What could she add to that?

"You sure you're okay?" Jake asked as he pulled into Clay Treasures' parking lot.

"I will be."

"I'm not so sure you should be heading off to Washington, but I'm not going to tell you not to go. What I am going to tell you is to be careful. Your ex-husband is dead. I'd hate for you to be next."

"I'll be careful."

"Seems your ex might have been more than just a murderer."

"What do you mean?"

"Two men came here tonight looking for something Cody said he gave you. Cody was killed three days ago. It could be someone has decided to go to a lot of trouble to make sure Cody never reveals what was on that disk."

"You think he was murdered to keep him quiet?"

"I don't know, but I plan to find out." Jake got out of the car and opened the door for Morgan, waiting as she climbed out. "The apartment should be clean. I told the crew to take care of that first. It may be a while longer before they finish in the gallery."

"That's fine."

"You go on up to your apartment. I'll wait here until the cleaning crew is done, and then lock up. There'll be a marked patrol car parked outside tonight, so don't worry that you won't be safe."

"Thank you, Sheriff Reed. I really appreciate it."

"No need to thank me. I'll see you tomorrow." He held the gallery door open, and Morgan walked in, frowning as she saw the carnage. Clay vases and pots had been smashed. A slick, wet spot stained the tile floor. All Morgan's hard work, all the time she'd spent creating a gallery that matched her dreams, and this is what it had come to.

"You'll get it back the way it was," the sheriff said quietly, and Morgan nodded.

Maybe she would. Or maybe she'd take the destruction of her gallery as a sign that it was time to move on.

A sign?

She didn't believe in signs. She believed in well thought out plans and carefully considered options. At least, that was what she used to believe in.

She sighed, waving to two women who were sweeping up shards of pottery, and hurried up the stairs to the apartment. The door was cracked open, and she gave it a gentle push, bracing herself for whatever she might see on the other side.

The coffee table had been righted. Someone had thrown pillows over ragged tears in the sofa, and Morgan could barely see the slashed fabric. The kitchen had been scrubbed clean, all the evidence of the brutal attack swept away. The ugliness of it still seemed to hang in the air, the choking fear and vicious pain of the time she'd spent trapped in her apartment seeping into Morgan's pores as she checked the den and the bedroom.

Maybe she *should* have stayed at Lacey's place for the night.

Morgan made another circuit of the house, checking the locks on the window and pulling the bolt on the door. Since she'd come to Lakeview, she'd been lax about keeping the apartment door locked. Mostly because she always locked the gallery below.

No more. If she returned to Clay Treasures after her trip to Washington, she'd never again sleep with the apartment door unlocked.

If?

When.

She *would* return to Lakeview and her pottery gallery. Cody had caused her enough pain and heartache. No way would she allow him to take away the dream she'd worked so hard to achieve. She frowned and walked into her bedroom. A large window looked out over the parking lot, and she hurried to close the curtains, blocking out the darkness beyond.

She should grab her laptop and boot it up, buy a plane ticket and pack her bags. She should do a lot of things, but all she wanted to do was lie in bed, close her eyes and forget that she'd almost been killed, forget that it had taken a stranger to save her life.

Forget that Cody was dead.

She blinked back hot tears and closed her eyes, wishing she *could* forget. As much as Cody had hurt and betrayed her, as much as she'd resented him, there'd been a time when she'd truly believed she would love him forever.

She sighed.

Cody was dead, but she was alive. There had to be a reason for that, and she wouldn't waste the second chance she'd been given.

She glanced at the alarm clock on the bedside table. It was midnight in Lakeview, but only nine in Spokane, Washington. Morgan took a deep breath, lifted the phone and dialed her parents' number.

FOUR

Jackson loosened his tie as he stepped out of the sanctuary and joined the crowd lining up to offer Jude and Lacey congratulations. The wedding seemed to have gone off without a hitch, but it wasn't the beautiful bride or peacock-proud groom that Jackson was anxious to speak with. Morgan was several guests ahead of him in line, her bruised jaw and swollen lip only partially camouflaged by makeup. Despite the obvious injuries, she walked with her head up and her shoulders back, her quick stride seeming to dare people to take a second look.

For his part, Jackson didn't need a dare to want to look again. Glossy black hair, pale blue eyes, slender figure encased in a curve-hugging dress. Even without the bruises, she was an attention grabber. What man wouldn't take a second look?

As he watched, Morgan offered Lacey a hug, said something to Jude and then hurried toward the exit. Jackson stepped out of line and followed. He and Jude had spoken at length before the wedding, and Jackson knew what his friend expected. Twenty-four-hour guard until the men who'd attacked Morgan were caught. Jackson didn't have a problem with that, but he was pretty sure Morgan would.

The day had the crisp, cold feel of late fall, the clear blue sky and bright sunlight belying any danger that might lurk nearby. Jackson followed Morgan across the parking lot, wondering if she realized how vulnerable she was. Despite the nearly overflowing parking lot and the buzzing crowd of people exiting the church, Morgan made an easy target. Buildings, trees and even cars were perfect hiding places for a sniper, and she was doing nothing to escape notice, nothing to keep her out of the line of fire.

He picked up his pace, reaching Morgan's side as she opened the door of a beat-up Chevy.

"Heading over to the reception?"

She jumped, whirling to face him. "Jackson, what are you doing here?"

"Same thing you are. Attending a friend's wedding."

"You know that's not what I mean."

"If you're asking why I'm standing here talking to you, I'd think the answer was obvious. I'm following through on a promise to a friend."

"You weren't serious about that."

"About making sure you stay safe until Jude and Lacey get back from France? Sure I am."

For a moment she said nothing, then she shook her head, her eyes flashing with amusement. "I've got to admit, I'm surprised. I thought it was all just an elaborate scheme to put Lacey at ease."

"I don't lie and I rarely scheme. Especially not when it comes to people who trust me. Lacey and Jude are both concerned about you. If it helps them feel more at ease, helps them enjoy their wedding and honeymoon, I've got every intention of following through on my promise to keep you safe."

"That's going to be difficult to do, considering that I'm going to be in Washington."

"Not so difficult if I'm in Washington with you."

"But you won't be. My plane leaves in an hour and a half,

and I've got to get going or I'll miss it," she said, shifting in her seat and closing the door.

Jackson didn't bother trying to stop her. No way did he think she'd change her mind and invite him along on the trip. Then again, there was no way he was going to break his word to Jude. He'd told his friend that he'd keep Morgan safe. That's exactly what he planned to do. Whether she liked it or not.

He crossed the parking lot and hopped into his Mustang, reaching for his cell phone as he pulled onto the road behind Morgan's car. He'd planned on returning to New York on Sunday, but his plans had changed and his boss was going to have to be informed. He dialed quickly, waiting impatiently for Kane Dougherty to pick up. Owner of Information Unlimited, Kane had founded the business two years ago and pulled Jackson on board shortly after.

"Dougherty here."

"It's Jackson."

"I thought you were at a friend's wedding."

"It's over."

"And you felt compelled to check in with me?"

"I ran into some trouble."

"If you're going to ask me to bail you out, forget it. I've got plans."

"No need to post bail, but I'm not going to be back Monday like I'd planned. I've got some personal business to take care of."

"When will you be back?" Kane asked, not demanding further detail. That was no surprise. Kane was a tenacious investigator but never stuck his nose into his employees' business.

"A week or two."

"You going to be able to work the cases you've been assigned, or should I call someone in to cover for you?"

"There's nothing on my docket that I can't work on long-distance," Jackson responded as he pulled into the airport parking lot and followed Morgan to the long-term parking garage. If she knew he was following, she gave no indication of it, just drove slowly through the crowded lot until she found an empty spot.

"That's fine then. I may have another case for you this week. You want it, or do you want me to pass it on to Skylar?"

"It depends on the case."

"It's another missing person case. A mother looking for a son she lost contact with a dozen years ago. Lady has just been diagnosed with cancer."

"I should be able to handle things from Washington."

"Washington?"

"I'm flying there in an hour."

"Check in with me Tuesday. I'll update you on the new case then."

"Sounds good. Talk to you then." Jackson hung up and pulled into a parking spot a half dozen yards away from Morgan. She seemed completely oblivious to his presence as she yanked a small rolling carry-on case from the trunk of her car and started walking toward the airport terminal.

Jackson had a feeling she wasn't. She'd survived a brutal attack, escaped two armed men. There was no way she didn't realize she'd been followed from the church.

He covered the distance between them quickly, saw her tense as he matched pace with her shorter stride.

"Need some help with the bag?"

"No. And I'd appreciate it if you'd stop following me." She didn't bother looking his way, just kept focusing straight ahead, her silky hair swinging as she moved. It was touchable hair. The kind Jackson could imagine running his fingers through if he let himself.

"That would make it a little difficult for me to do my job."

"You don't have a job. At least not one that involves me."

"I guess we'll have to agree to disagree on that," he said, smiling as she glared in his direction.

"Has anyone ever told you that you're infuriating?"

"My sister used to."

"She doesn't anymore?"

"If she were still alive she probably would." And after two and a half years, the truth of her death was as fresh and ugly as it had been the day Jackson had learned that his older sister had been murdered.

"I'm sorry. I didn't realize…"

"How could you have?"

She shrugged, her hair brushing against the slim column of her neck. Dark, oversize sunglasses hid her eyes but did little to draw attention away from her bruises. They were dark blue and green against her tan skin, and Jackson wanted to take her to the nearest hospital and make sure she stayed there until she recovered. "I'm still sorry. You must miss her a lot."

"I do. Lindsey was a great person," Jackson said, knowing that words could never adequately describe his oldest sister. Sweet, funny and intelligent, she'd loved passionately and without reservation. In the end, it was love that had been her undoing.

"Were the two of you close?"

"Not as much in the few years before her death, but when we were kids, we were."

"I guess that makes it harder."

"It does, but I realized a few months after she died that I could drown in regret or I could learn from my mistakes and move on." Learning had been the easy part. It was the moving on that Jackson was still having trouble with.

"It takes two people to make a relationship strong, so I'm sure you weren't the only one at fault for the distance between you and your sister," Morgan said as she tried to maneuver her carry-on over a curb. She grimaced, releasing the case and grabbing her side.

Jackson put a hand on her shoulder, holding her steady as she caught her breath. He could feel delicate bones and tense muscles beneath her jacket, could feel her arm tremble as she shifted beneath his touch. He wanted to tell her everything would be okay, that he'd make sure of it, but he doubted she'd want to hear it. He grabbed her carry-on instead, ignoring her sputtered protest.

"You should be home in bed, Morgan. Not traveling to Washington."

"You might be right, but I'm going anyway. It's been a long time since I've been to visit my parents. Too long."

"It won't hurt to wait a few days, give yourself a chance to heal."

"It will if…."

"What?"

"Nothing."

He let it go. She didn't have to finish the thought for Jackson to know what she was thinking. If the men who'd attacked her got their hands on her again, she might be out of chances to visit family and reconnect with those she loved. "Do your parents know you're going back home?"

"Know? I left a message on their answering machine, and they've called me ten times to make sure I haven't changed my mind. If my father had his way, he'd be heading here to play escort."

"That might not have been such a bad idea."

"I'm about fifteen years too old to need an escort. Besides, by the time he returned my call, I'd already booked my flight. There was no way he could get here before I took off." She smiled wanly, pulling off her sunglasses as they stepped into the airport. "Speaking of which, my plane boards in an hour, and I'm going to wait by the boarding gate until then."

"Is that a subtle hint that this is good-bye?"

"I wouldn't call it a hint, and I'm sure it wasn't very subtle. But I didn't sleep much last night, and I'd rather sit and be quiet than stand and chat," she said, brushing a few strands of inky hair from her cheek, the sleeve of her jacket riding up to reveal blue-gray smudges circling her wrist.

An image flashed through Jackson's mind. Lindsey the last time he'd seen her. The deep black bruises on her neck. The tubes that had snaked from her broken body. The pale, lifeless face that had once been vibrant and filled with humor. "Be careful, Morgan. The men who attacked you last night are still on the loose."

"Believe me, I know it. It's pretty much all I've thought about for the past twelve hours."

"Did you speak with Jake this morning?"

"Briefly. He called me a few hours before the wedding to let me know that he contacted the Spokane Police Department. They know I'm on the way. Other than that, he didn't have much to report."

"No leads?"

"None that he was willing to share."

"I'll make some phone calls. See if any of my old pals in the New York City Police Department have information about your ex's murder."

"I'm sure that Jake is already taking care of that."

"I'm sure he is, too, but I don't think he'd frown on another set of eyes and ears. Besides, I've got some buddies on the force. They may be willing to share information with me that they wouldn't with someone else."

"Even if it's information that can help break a case?"

"The information I'm talking about is more the specula-tive type."

"You mean gossip," she said, moving toward the Northwest Airlines gate.

"Gossiping wouldn't be a very manly thing to do. I prefer to think of it as dispersal of unproven information."

"Dispersal of unproven information, huh? I'll have to remember that one." They'd reached the gate, and Morgan stopped, turning to face Jackson. With the dark glasses off, Jackson could clearly see the fear and worry in her eyes. "I know it may seem like I'm not grateful to you for what you've done, but I am. You saved my life, and I don't take that lightly."

"You saved your own life, Morgan. I just happened to be there to help out."

"That's nice of you to say, but I think we both know the truth," she said, reaching for his hand and squeezing it.

The jolt of awareness that shot through him was as unexpected as it was unwelcome.

Surprised, he met her eyes, saw his own shock reflected there.

She dropped his hand, took a quick step back. "Take care, Jackson."

She hurried away before he could respond.

That was fine. He'd ignore what he'd felt. Chalk it up to fatigue and stress or too many months out of the dating game. What he wouldn't do was let Morgan travel to Washington alone. She was in too vulnerable a condition. If she ran into her enemies again, she'd have no way to defend herself. No hope of escape.

He watched until she was through the security gate, and then he followed, trying to blend in with an older couple moving into the boarding area ahead of him. No sense in letting Morgan know he'd booked a flight to Spokane until it was too late for either of them to trade in their tickets.

Morgan was a hundred yards away, sitting with her back to the security gate. Not a good move. Anyone could walk through without her noticing. Jackson was tempted to tell her that, but figured it could wait. They'd have plenty of time to talk about safety measures on the flight to Spokane.

He took a seat on a bench several rows away from Morgan, positioning himself so that he was partially hidden by an information desk. They'd board the plane in a half hour. That would be soon enough to let Morgan know he was sticking around. He was pretty sure she wouldn't be happy about it, and he was just as sure he didn't care. He'd made the mistake of believing Lindsey when she'd brushed off his concern over a bruised cheek and a broken finger. An accident, she'd said. And he'd taken her at her word. Two months later, she was dead.

God knew Jackson regretted not asking more questions, regretted not allowing himself to imagine the unimaginable.

Regretted it, but regret didn't change what had happened, and it couldn't bring his sister back.

He was going to Spokane. He was going to finish what he'd started because he had to.

For Lindsey.

For Lacey and Jude.

For Morgan.

And maybe, more than anything else, for himself.

FIVE

Home.

That was the word Jackson had used to describe Spokane, but it wasn't the word Morgan would use to describe the place where she'd spent thirteen years of her life. It wasn't that Richard and Sue Alexandria hadn't tried to make Morgan feel like she was home. It was more that Morgan had always felt like an outsider. A bad apple in a basketful of good ones. Her parents had adopted three other children before Morgan came along and all of them had adjusted beautifully to their new lives. Morgan, on the other hand, had fought tooth and nail to maintain her independence and to preserve her identity.

She hadn't wanted to forget where she'd come from. Hadn't wanted to forget the siblings she'd left behind. Had vowed to find them again. By the time she was thirteen, she'd run away so many times and caused so much chaos in the Alexandrias' home that she'd been sent to spend the summer with her mother's sister. Aunt Helen lived in a modern mountain cabin far enough from civilization that running had been impossible. It was there that Morgan had learned to throw a pot rather than a tantrum, and during the four summers she'd spent with Helen, she'd finally settled down and settled in.

But she hadn't found home.

Maybe she never would.

The flight attendant called for economy class to board, and Morgan followed the line of passengers through the boarding bay and onto the plane. Her seat was in the rear, and she carried her bag through the narrow aisle, ignoring the not-so-subtle stares of the other travelers. Obviously, the makeup she'd piled on before Lacey's wedding wasn't doing its job. Neither was the Tylenol she'd swallowed before Lacey's wedding, but she didn't dare take the painkiller the doctor had prescribed. The last thing she wanted was to be knocked out cold while two men hunted her down.

She muscled her carry-on into the overhead compartment, scooted past a man already reclining in the aisle seat, and settled into the spot near the window, dropping her purse onto the floor near her feet. A young businessman maneuvered into the seat beside her, flipping open a financial magazine and reading it as more people filed past. The flight was full, and her seat had come at a premium after another passenger had cancelled, but Morgan was on the plane and safe.

That was something to be thankful for.

Unfortunately, she wouldn't stay safe for long if she didn't figure out why Cody had been killed.

A disk. That's what the men had wanted.

Which probably meant information.

Financial information?

Cody and his business partner Sean Macmillan had been financial advisers for some high-powered clients. Could one of them have had something to hide? Something that Cody was privy to?

"Excuse me, sir," a flight attendant said to the man seated beside Morgan. "Would you like to upgrade to first class?"

He shrugged, grabbed his things and followed the stewardess back up the aisle. Minutes later, the flight attendant returned, another passenger with her. Morgan glanced at the new arrival. Looked again.

Tall.

Rangy, muscular build.

Auburn hair.

Blue eyes staring into hers.

Jackson.

The man who'd saved her life.

She'd touched his hand and felt something she hadn't felt in a very long time. Something she'd told herself she would never feel again.

And now he was on the plane.

Sitting in the seat beside her.

She knew she should be angry that he'd followed her, but all she felt was vague surprise and the strange sense that she'd rather have him travel with her than travel alone.

Which wasn't the truth.

She had been going it alone since the day she'd walked out on Cody, and that was the way she liked it.

"All settled in? Looks like the flight is taking off on time," he said, acting as if they were on a trip they'd been planning together for years. Acting as if they'd *been* together for years.

"Not with both of us on it, it won't," she muttered, knowing there was nothing she could do about his presence. Not even sure she wanted to do anything about it.

And that worried her.

A lot.

"Are you planning on leaving?" he asked.

"No."

"Good. Because they've already closed the doors. We should be cleared to take off in a few minutes."

"I'm not even going to ask you why you're here or tell you you shouldn't be."

"There's no need, seeing as how we already discussed things before we boarded."

"Discussed things and decided that I didn't need you along for the ride."

"Actually, we didn't decide that. You said it. I listened."

"And then decided to do what you wanted?"

"Something like that."

"Well, you're wasting your time. It's not like I'm in imminent danger."

"Not now, but you may be while you wait for your connecting flight." He grabbed the end of his seatbelt, his knuckles brushing Morgan's hip. Heat shot through her, and she shifted, trying to put some distance between them.

She would *not* be attracted to Jackson. Loving Cody had taken everything she had and left her with nothing but a truck-load of sadness and resentment.

She wouldn't go through that again.

Couldn't go through it again.

"I don't plan to leave the airport, so I'm sure I'll be fine," she said, a moment too late, and he grinned as if he knew just how uncomfortable he made her.

"You may be right, but I'm not going to take any chances."

"Look, Jackson—"

"We can argue from now until the plane lands, but it won't change anything. I'm here. Why not just relax and let me help you?"

"Because I don't need help." But the words didn't sound nearly as convincing as she meant them to, and she turned to look out the window.

"Everyone needs help sometimes," he said quietly.

He was right, of course, and maybe he was right to think that Morgan was in over her head, that she needed whatever protection he could offer, but accepting that would mean accepting him, and Morgan couldn't allow herself to do it. "True, but right now, I really am fine. During my layover in Chicago, I'll sit in the terminal and wait. What could possibly happen in an airport filled with people?"

"My first case as a homicide detective, I investigated a murder that took place on the New York subway in broad daylight. Not one witness to be found."

"I'd forgotten you were a homicide detective."

"I didn't know you ever knew it," he said, settling more deeply into his seat, his legs stretched out beside Morgan's. He looked relaxed and comfortable.

Morgan felt crowded and ill at ease.

Being around Jackson reminded her of all the reasons she'd enjoyed being part of a couple. Companionship. Conversation. The feeling of belonging. Those were things she'd been almost desperate for when she'd met Cody. Now she was older, hopefully wiser, and having those things didn't seem nearly as important.

"Sheriff Reed mentioned it last night, and Lacey told me that you and Jude worked homicide together a few years back."

"I'm flattered that you remember." Jackson grinned, and Morgan's heart skipped a beat.

"Don't be. I've always had a good memory," she responded, refusing to look away. Her heart might respond to Jackson's charming smile, but *she* would not.

"A good memory should help."

"With?"

"Our investigation. I'm sure you realize that you won't be safe until we find the disk and figure out what's on it."

"*We* don't have to figure out anything. The Lakeview Sheriff's Department is investigating. I'm sure the New York police are, too." And she'd join them in the hunt for the disk. *After* she got rid of Jackson.

And she *would* get rid of him. She had enough trouble to deal with without worrying about Jackson and her reaction to him.

Reaction to Jackson?

She wasn't reacting to anything but fatigue, pain and fear.

At least that's what she was going to tell herself. It was that or acknowledge the unthinkable—attraction to a man who was just as handsome, just as charming, and just as likely to break her heart as Cody had been.

"I've got no doubt they're working hard to find answers, Morgan, but they don't have the inside scoop."

"Inside scoop?"

"You and your memory."

"I've already told the police everything I know."

"You'd be surprised how much can lurk just beneath conscious thought. If we dig hard enough, we're bound to find something interesting."

Everything he said was completely reasonable. Except the *we* part of it.

Morgan pulled a travel pack of pain reliever from her purse and ripped it open, too tired to argue. There'd be time enough to tell Jackson she didn't want him digging into her life after the plane landed.

"You okay?" Jackson laid a hand on her wrist, the contact shooting warmth up her arm.

"The problem with bruises is they always hurt worse the next day," she said, easing her arm away.

"I'll get the flight attendant to bring you some water." His hand dropped away, but the heat of it seemed to remain.

"And interrupt her safety spiel? I'll manage without." She tossed two tablets into her mouth and barely managed to swallow them down, their bitterness forging a hot trail down the back of her throat as the jet picked up speed and began its ascent. Outside, the world sped by, shape bleeding into shape, color into color until it was nothing but a smudged painting without outline or frame.

When Morgan returned to Lakeview, she'd throw a bowl, let

the clay slip between her palms and slicken her fingers. She could picture it in her mind, large and round with a smooth, wide lip. She'd glaze it with the same smudged colors that passed outside the plane's window. Blues and greens and gray. Splashes of white. When it was complete, she'd set in on the large table to the left of the gallery door. Maybe she'd sell it. Maybe not, but it would be there. Beautiful, real and solid in a way the world outside was not.

It was something to look forward to when she returned.

If she returned.

"Looks like we're on our way," Jackson said, his words carrying over the sound of the jet's engine and Morgan's echoing thoughts.

"Looks like it."

"You don't seem all that happy to be going home."

"Spokane isn't home."

"Then where is?"

"I'm not sure I've figured that out yet," she said without thinking.

"No?"

"Or maybe I should say that I've had so many of them in my life, I haven't decided which one I should claim as mine."

"Now I'm curious."

"Why?"

"I've never met someone who couldn't identify a particular place as home," he said, studying her with an intensity that made her feel as if they were alone, two people with all the time in the world to get to know one another.

But Morgan didn't want to get to know Jackson, and she certainly didn't want him to get to know her. She needed to keep her distance and guard her heart, or she might find herself in a place she didn't want to be.

"There are millions of people just like me, Jackson. Not

everyone grows up with loving, stable parents, you know. Not everyone comes home to fresh-baked cookies and help with her homework."

"Sounds like you didn't have much of a childhood."

"Let's just say I grew up quickly, and change the subject. I don't enjoy talking about the past."

"I'm sorry to hear that, because if we're going to figure out where Cody hid that disk, we're going to have to talk about it a lot."

"For all I know, Cody never had a disk."

"You think he'd lie?"

"If he thought he could protect himself by doing so, sure," she offered, happy to turn the conversation away from herself.

"Even if it meant throwing you to the wolves?"

"If you insist on investigating Cody, you're going to find out pretty quickly what it took me nearly six years to discover. Cody's biggest concern was himself. If he were in enough danger, he'd throw his mother to the wolves."

"Then I guess the question we need to ask is—what was it he was trying to protect himself from?"

"Or who?"

"That, too. Did he have enemies?"

"Probably as many as he had friends. Cody collected people, used them and then discarded them."

"He sounds like a great guy."

"Yeah. He was. Now, if you don't mind, I've got a splitting headache, and I'm going to rest my eyes for a while," she said, quickly closing her eyes and shutting out Jackson's rugged face and blazing blue-gold gaze.

He was right, of course. Morgan was going to have to dig into the past, think about Cody and try to figure out where he'd hidden the disk. She'd known that since she'd walked out of the hospital the previous night. What she didn't have to do was discuss things with a stranger.

A stranger who seemed as familiar as an old friend.

If she let herself, Morgan could imagine sharing more than facts with Jackson. She could imagine telling him about the years she'd spent desperately trying to make her marriage work, could imagine sharing the grief she'd felt when she'd first realized that the man she loved had never really loved her.

But in that direction lay danger.

Jackson shifted, and Morgan opened her eyes, realized that he'd leaned close, was studying her face with an intensity that stole her breath.

"What are you doing?" she asked, her throat tight with emotions she refused to acknowledge.

"Wondering if I should ask the flight attendant for an ice pack for your jaw. It looks like the swelling has gotten worse." He touched her jaw lightly, his fingers cool against hot, swollen flesh.

"I don't think an ice pack is going to help at this point," she responded, pulling away from his touch.

"It might take the swelling down."

"The swelling is the least of my worries," she said, shifting in her seat and trying to put a little more distance between them.

"If you keep moving away from me, you'll burrow a hole in the side of the plane."

"I'm not moving away from you," she lied. "I'm trying to get comfortable."

"I see."

"What?"

"I'm making you nervous."

"Why would you think that?"

"Just a feeling I've got."

"Well, your feeling is wrong. You're not making me nervous. You're crowding me."

"I've got a choice between crowding you and crowding the guy next to me. I think I'm going to have to stick with you."

"I'm sure the guy beside you appreciates it," Morgan muttered, closing her eyes again.

Continuing her conversation with Jackson wasn't a good idea. Jackson Sharo was trouble, and the sooner she got him out of her life the better.

In two hours, they'd land at the Chicago airport, and that was where she and Jackson would part company. He'd saved her life, and maybe he was genuinely concerned for her well-being, but Morgan had been taking care of herself for a long time. She had no intention of changing that now.

Once they landed, she'd explain that to her unwanted companion. No doubt he'd be reasonable and agree to get on the next plane back to Lakeview, and she'd be relieved to see him go.

Sure you will.

The thought floated through Morgan's mind, and she frowned, opening her eyes and focusing on the blue sky outside the window. The past twenty-four hours had been tough, but she was a survivor. First as a young girl living in poverty and neglect. Then as an orphan fighting for her place in the orphanage. Now, as an adult facing her husband's infidelity, his crime and his death. Survivors didn't quit. They didn't give in. And they certainly didn't sit around hoping someone else would save them.

She'd better keep that in mind, because if she didn't, she just might relax and let Jackson take control of everything. And that, she knew, would only lead to heartache.

SIX

Danger hovered just out of sight. Watching. Waiting. Hoping for an opportunity to strike. Jackson couldn't see it, but he could feel it staring daggers into his back as he pulled Morgan's carry-on case through the crowded Chicago airport. He lowered the handle of the case and lifted it. Easier to carry the case than to drag it through the crowd. Easier and quicker.

"Well, we made it," Morgan said, with a false cheerfulness that Jackson didn't miss. Could she sense the danger that seemed to hang in the air?

Maybe. Maybe not. Either way, Jackson knew what she wanted—him gone.

She wasn't the only one. Whoever was watching was probably hoping for the same thing. Alone, Morgan was no match for the kind of men who'd attacked her. They knew it. Jackson knew it. The only one who didn't seem to know it was Morgan.

"The question is, did the guys who are after you make it, too?" Jackson responded.

"Even if they knew what plane I was on, they'd have had to take a different flight out."

"Maybe. I got a ticket. It's possible they did, too. We have to think of all the possibilities, Morgan. And plan for them," Jackson said, his gaze focused on the people waiting outside the departure gate. Family and friends, people going about their daily lives, excited and happy to be greeting loved ones.

Was someone else waiting?

Someone hoping to get a chance to speak with Morgan again? There was no doubt where such a meeting would lead. Whether they got what they wanted or not, they'd kill her.

"I agree. That's why I'm going to find my connecting flight and stay by the boarding gate until it's time to leave. Once I get on the plane to Spokane, I'll be fine. Sheriff Reed said he's informed the police there of my arrival, and I'm sure they'll be there to look out for me." She hedged around the issue of whether or not Jackson would continue the journey with her.

Jackson had expected her to begin arguing her points as soon as the plane touched the ground, doing her best to convince him to go back to Lakeview. She hadn't. Maybe she was feeling exactly what he was. A pump of adrenaline, a hum of awareness, a silent warning that trouble was nearby.

He slipped an arm around her waist, pulling her to his side and holding tight when she would have pulled away. "Let's stick close for a while, okay?"

"Close? We're nearly joined at the hip," she huffed, but she didn't try to move away again. The scent of her perfume swirled around them. Light and subtle with an exotic undertone, it matched its wearer perfectly. It was something Jackson shouldn't be noticing. Not when there was so much at stake.

He frowned, hurrying Morgan toward the arrival gate.

"Are you leaving?" Morgan asked, as if she really believed he would.

"*We're* leaving. I thought we'd go get something to eat."

"I appreciate the thought, but I'm not hungry."

"I'm not, either," he responded, glancing around as he stepped into the busy terminal. The place was teaming with people, and if any of them were watching Morgan and Jackson, they weren't being obvious about it.

"Then why…." Her voice trailed off, and her eyes widened. "You think they're here."

She didn't say who "they" were. She didn't have to. They both knew.

They were the men who'd beaten her, who'd do worse if they got their hands on her again.

"I think there's a possibility they're here. I figure we'll walk outside, get in a cab and see if anyone follows. That should confirm or allay my suspicions."

"Go outside and get a cab? Are you kidding? That's like waving a red flag in front of a bull."

"I was thinking of it more as baiting a rat trap."

"And we're the bait?"

"If it brings our perps out of hiding, it'll be worth it," he said, not releasing his hold as he led Morgan outside into the cool fall day.

"I hope you have a plan for when the bull decides to charge."

Dark clouds hung over the sky, trapping the scent of the exhaust that wafted from the mufflers of a dozen taxis that idled nearby.

Jackson urged Morgan to one of them, glancing over his shoulder as the driver opened the door and then the trunk. Several dozen people had walked out of the airport. A couple. A family. A woman alone. None of them looked like the kind of danger Jackson was expecting.

And he *was* expecting it.

Someone had killed Cody in an attempt to retrieve the disk he'd hidden. Had it been an act of desperation or an act of cold calculation? The disk was worth a lot to someone, and whoever wanted it believed Morgan knew where it was.

He tossed the carry-on into the trunk and got into the taxi, positioning himself so that he had a clear view out the back and side windows.

"Where to?" the driver asked.

"Know a good place to eat around here?"

"There's a diner a couple of miles away. Good food. Quick service."

"Sounds perfect," Jackson said, his attention focused on the door they'd just exited through.

Come on. I know you're in there. Just step outside and let me get a look before we drive off.

As if his thoughts had conjured them, three men exited the building. One was dressed in a business suit and hurried toward a waiting cab. The other two surveyed the area, their casual attire and relaxed demeanor hinting of nothing beyond what they seemed to be. There was something about them that drew Jackson's attention, though. Something that didn't seem right. Maybe it was the stealthy, fluid way they moved. Or maybe it was the way they seemed to avoid looking in Jackson's direction. He caught just a glimpse of their profiles before the taxi pulled into traffic exiting the airport and he lost sight of them.

Had they gotten in a cab?

He'd find out soon enough. If they were the guys who'd attacked Morgan, they'd follow. To the diner, to Spokane, to anyplace where they thought Morgan and the disk might be found.

"Did someone follow us?" Morgan asked, shifting in her seat so that she could look out the back window. Watery sunlight filtered through the taxi's window, bathing Morgan's face in blue-gray light and adding depth to the bruises that tracked along her jaw and her cheek.

She had a tough, sharp-edged personality, but there was a fragility beneath it that made Jackson want to tuck her away in a safe house until she was out of danger.

Of course, if he tried, she'd fight him, kicking and scream-ing the entire way.

"I saw a couple of men walk out of the airport," Jackson said.

"I saw a couple of dozen people walk out of the airport. What was different about the two you noticed?"

"Nothing I can put my finger on, but it won't hurt to see if they follow us."

"And if they do? What then?"

"We'll call in the police and have them questioned."

"Before or after they pull guns and shoot us?"

Her comment surprised a smile out of Jackson, and he patted her knee, realizing too late the mistake he was making.

Heat shot through him at the contact, and he pulled away, irritated with his reaction. He'd worked plenty of cases since he joined Kane Dogherty's PI firm, Information Unlimited, had had other clients as beautiful and compelling as Morgan. None of them had affected him the way she did.

He took a deep, steadying breath, forced himself to focus on the conversation. "If they're the men from last night, they flew in from Virginia. No way are they carrying guns."

"I hadn't thought of that. I suppose it's something to be thankful for. Although I think I'd rather be shot than stabbed. It seems like a faster way to die."

"Depends on where the wound is. I've investigated homicide cases that involved a knife wound directly to the heart or neck. It's amazing how quickly that can kill a person."

"Thanks for that image, Jackson. I'm sure it'll help me sleep tonight."

"Sorry. I forgot I was talking to a delicate flower of a woman," he said, grinning as she scowled.

"'Delicate flower of a woman.' You're one of those kinds of men, aren't you?"

"What kind of man would that be?"

"The kind that flashes a charming smile and gets what he wants?"

"I'd like to say that's how I *used* to be," he responded lightly. He'd changed a lot since Lindsey died. Become more serious. Less playful. Started to yearn for something permanent and strong. Like what his parents had and what he'd always said he didn't want.

"You'd *like* to say it?"

"I guess it's up to other people to decide whether or not I've changed," he responded absently, his gaze on the traffic behind them as the taxi driver pulled into the parking lot of a small diner.

"Here we are, folks. You want me to come pick you up in an hour? I can take you back to the airport or to your hotel or wherever you're staying."

"How much would it cost for you to wait here?" Jackson asked, his eyes on a taxi that had stopped a block away from the diner.

"Normal rate. You pay by the minute."

"Do you know if this place has a back entrance?"

"Can't say I do, but seems like it would be fire code."

"I'll give you a hundred bucks to drive a couple blocks away, then circle back here. Pull around to the back and wait for us there."

"A hundred bucks plus my regular fare?" the driver asked, his eyes gleaming with anticipation.

"Sure."

"It's your nickel, then. Pay me for this trip up front, though. I don't want to be stiffed."

Jackson handed him a few crumbled bills and then got out and grabbed Morgan's carry-on from the trunk.

She was out of the taxi and beside him before he got the trunk closed.

"You think they followed us, don't you?" she asked, and he nodded.

"There's a taxi a block up, idling near the curb. Don't bother looking for it. We don't want them to realize they've been spotted."

"We'd better call the police."

"We will, but I want to see if I can get a look at our guys first."

"Just in case the police don't get here before they leave?"

"Exactly."

"Good plan. So let's get it done," she responded, marching toward the diner like a prisoner going to the gallows.

She wasn't the delicate flower he'd teased her about earlier, but not quite the hardened cynic she'd probably like people to believe she was, either.

So who was she?

Jackson wasn't sure, but he planned to find out. There was something about Morgan that appealed to him. Maybe it was her fierce independence, which was so different from the neediness of most of the women he'd dated. Or maybe it was the vulnerability he sensed beneath the surface. Maybe it was simply that he'd helped save her life and wanted to make sure she continued to survive.

Whatever the case, he planned to find out more about Morgan Alexandria.

But first, he needed to find out more about the men who had almost killed her.

SEVEN

Morgan was sure she felt the weight of a hundred eyes following as she made her way to the entrance of the diner and pushed open the door. She wanted to turn around, study her surroundings and try to find the source of the uncomfortable feeling, but Jackson was right. If she looked, she'd be tempted to search for the taxi he'd spotted. The last thing she wanted was to give up the advantage she and Jackson had.

She stepped inside the dimly lit diner, Jackson just a few feet behind. She didn't need to look to know he was there. Didn't need to have him close to feel his presence. His scent had enveloped her on the flight to the Chicago airport, his spicy, masculine cologne filling her senses until she'd been tempted to get up and walk the length of the cabin just to get away from him.

Men.

Who needed them?

She didn't. That's for sure.

She'd sworn off them the night she'd unpacked Cody's suitcase and found another woman's lingerie. He'd had an excuse, of course. He always did. A mix-up with the hotel laundry, he'd said, and had even called to complain. The problem was, for the first time in their marriage Morgan hadn't been able to believe the lie.

"Table for two?" a cheerful waitress asked, interrupting Morgan's unhappy thoughts.

"Can we get one near a front window?" Jackson responded with a smile that would have made Morgan's heart melt if it hadn't been icy cold and carved from the reality of Cody's infidelity.

"Whatever you want." The waitress offered a smile of her own and a quick wink aimed at Jackson before she led them to a booth with a view of the front parking lot and handed them each a menu.

As soon as she left, Morgan leaned close to the window, trying to see up the street. "Do you think they're out there?"

"I think we're going to find out soon, so how about we decide what we want to eat before they show up."

"Eat? How can you possibly be thinking of food at a time like this?"

"Easily. I haven't eaten since breakfast, and I'm hungry. I'm going to have a turkey club. I'll order the same for you."

"I…" She was going to say she didn't want anything, but what was the point in arguing? The fact was, they had a long day ahead of them. Facing it with a full stomach was probably a better idea then facing it with an empty one. Even if doing so meant choking down the food while being stalked by two men who probably wanted her dead.

"That's fine."

Jackson waved the waitress over and ordered the food to go, then turned his attention back to the parking lot. If he was anxious it didn't show. His body was relaxed, his hands splayed out on the table, tapping a beat on the scarred wood. He looked like what he was—a handsome, confident professional who probably had a full life beyond his business dealings. So why wasn't he rushing back to New York? What had he been thinking when he'd offered to protect Morgan while Jude and Lacey honeymooned?

Maybe he hadn't been thinking at all. Maybe the offer had simply been a means to an end. He wanted his good friend to have a wonderful wedding and honeymoon, and he'd said whatever was necessary to make sure that happened. A Cody-like move by a man who was too much like Morgan's ex-husband for her peace of mind.

And nothing like him at all. After all, Jackson had followed through on his promise. Had gone out of his way to do what he'd said he would.

Morgan frowned, not liking the direction of her thoughts, and turned her attention back to the parking lot. "See anything yet?"

"I think so."

"Who? Where?"

"Look up the road. See the two guys walking toward the diner?"

"Jeans and T-shirts, and one is wearing a baseball cap?"

"They just got out of the cab, and I think they're the guys I saw at the airport. Neither was wearing a hat then, but they carry themselves the same. Do you recognize either of them?"

Did she?

Morgan peered out the window, trying to get a better look. The previous night was a blur, the pain and shock of what had happened wiping out some of the memories, but not all of them. She remembered the moment the men had entered her shop. Confident and sure of themselves, moving with a stealthy ease that had put Morgan on edge. If only she'd run up the stairs and to her apartment as soon as she'd seen them, she might have saved herself a whole lot of pain. She wouldn't have needed Jackson to save her, and she'd still be in Lakeview, enjoying the last few moments of Lacey's wedding.

Or she'd have been chased up the stairs, her door would have been broken down and she'd still be right where she was, staring out the window at two men who actually did look vaguely familiar. "It could be them, but both have blond hair. One of the guys last night was a brunette."

"Hair color can be changed."

"I know. It's just so hard to say for sure. Everything happened so fast. One minute I was standing behind the counter, wrapping a pot that a client was going to pick up today, the next I was lying on the floor." She'd come to in her kitchen, cold water dripping down her face, her head throbbing with pain. There'd been more pain to come, but Morgan preferred not to dwell on it. She'd survived being abandoned by her birth mother and a year in a Latvian orphanage by refusing to acknowledge the hunger and the desperation she'd felt as she lay on a hard wooden pallet every night. She'd survived being separated from her brother and sister by refusing to feel the pain that had ripped at her heart and torn at her stomach.

Or trying to refuse it.

Letting go of the pain of losing Nikolai and Katia had been as impossible as assimilating into the Alexandria family. Nearly twenty years later, and she was still trying unsuccessfully to do both.

"You still with me?" Jackson asked, his hand covering hers, his palm pressed against her knuckles, the touch more comforting than she wanted it to be.

"Yes, I'm just trying to remember." She needed to focus. *Were* the men the same ones who'd attacked her the night before?

She watched as they drew nearer, focusing on the way they moved, the angle of their jaws, the shape of their noses and eyes. They didn't look like the kind of men who'd be up to no good, but there was something about their hard expressions that made Morgan shiver. "I think it's them."

"How sure are you?"

"Eighty percent."

"That won't hold up in a court of law, but it's good enough

for me. Looks like we're not going to get to eat after all." He clasped her hand and stood, tugging her through the diner. "Let's see where that corridor marked Restrooms leads. Maybe we'll get lucky and find a back way out of this place."

"Then what?"

"Call the police to come question our friends. While they're being questioned, we'll find a safe place to stay until we figure out what's going on."

"I've got a plane to catch in less than two hours," Morgan responded, her skin crawling, her mind shouting *danger.* She'd survived the previous night, and she had no desire to repeat the experience.

"Do you really want to do what they're expecting?" Jackson asked as he tugged her into a short corridor. An exit signed glowed at the far end, and Morgan wanted to rip away from Jackson and run for it.

"No, but I really want to see my family." It had been too long since she'd visited, too many days since she'd called her parents just to say hi. Despite what she'd said to Jackson, there was a part of her that longed to call their pretty ranch-style house home.

"I think your parents would rather have you alive and somewhere safe than with them and in danger," Jackson responded, his hand still wrapped around hers as he pushed open the exit door. Watery sunlight splashed onto scarred pavement, but did little to warm Morgan. She felt chilled and scared. The terror of the moment mixing with the terrors of the past. A hodgepodge of feelings that she needed to ignore if she were going to escape.

"I guess you've got an idea of where 'safe' is."

"Anywhere they won't expect," he said, scanning the littered back lot of the diner and smiling as he saw their taxi parked near the corner of the building. "Looks like our taxi driver wanted that extra hundred bucks."

"I hope you've got it on you, because I'm all out of cash."

"Not a problem. I like to be prepared when I travel." He held the taxi door open for her and she eased into the seat, sliding over so that he could climb in after her.

"You two want to go back to the airport?" the driver asked, his dark eyes meeting Morgan's in the rearview mirror. Was he curious about her bruises? Wondering if maybe she and Jackson were criminals? Maybe wondering if he was getting himself in deeper than a hundred dollars could dig him out of?

"Sounds good."

"You got my hundred bucks first?"

Jackson pulled a hundred-dollar bill from his pocket, frowning when the driver held it up to the light and studied it.

"It's good."

"Yeah? Then you won't mind me taking a careful look before we go."

"Actually, we've got a flight to catch," Morgan cut in, her gaze on the back door of the diner. Despite what Jackson had said about the men not having guns, she expected the door to fly open and bullets to roar from the barrels of guns. She expected the taxi driver and Jackson to die and herself to be kidnapped at gunpoint.

Please, Lord, get this guy moving, she prayed, not sure God heard. Not completely convinced He cared enough to answer even if He did. She wanted to believe, though, and maybe in that desire lay the beginning of the faith she'd always longed for but had never quite achieved.

"Looks good," the driver muttered, shoving the bill into his pocket and starting the engine.

Morgan's stomach twisted with sick dread as the taxi pulled around and passed close to door. Was it her imagination or was it opening?

She pivoted in her seat, trying to get a better look as the driver drove around the corner of the building.

"Relax. They know we've spotted them, and they'll probably

do their best to disappear before the police arrive," Jackson whispered, his lips so close to Morgan's ear she could feel the warmth of his breath on her skin. She shivered. Not from fear this time, but something else just as visceral and unwanted.

She shifted, trying to put distance between them, her gaze still focused out the back window, her mind screaming that she'd better be very careful around Jackson.

If he sensed her discomfort, he didn't show it. Just pulled out his cell phone and dialed. "Sheriff Reed? Jackson Sharo."

Surprised, Morgan turned her attention back to Jackson, wondering why he'd called a police officer in a different city. Wouldn't it have been better to call 911?

As if he sensed her thoughts, Jackson met Morgan's eyes and smiled. "We're fine, but it looks like we may have been followed. Two men. Midtwenties. Clean-cut. Blond hair. Military looking. One's about six feet. The other is five-ten. Eye color unknown." He paused, looking at Morgan again, listening to whatever it was Sheriff Reed said in reply.

"No, she doesn't have a very clear memory of things. I've got the address where the suspects were last seen. Ready?" He rattled it off, listened for another minute.

"I agree. They'll probably head back to the airport. I think the police should head there. We're flying out in an hour and a half. I'm confident they'll try to follow us there. Thanks for your help on this." He said good-bye and hung up the phone.

"Wouldn't it have been easier to call nine-one-one? You could have saved time that way. Gotten the police here involved and then called Sheriff Reed," Morgan said, her body humming with adrenaline and fear. She'd realized soon after marrying him that Cody was trouble. She just hadn't realized how much trouble. Cheating and lying were bad enough, but sending cold-blooded killers after Morgan was something she wouldn't have expected even from him.

Which, she supposed, proved just how well she'd known the man she'd once thought she would spend the rest of her life with.

"The police would have wanted to call Jake to verify my story, so it was easier to have him call them with the information."

"Do you think the men are still at the diner?"

"I doubt it. I figured they'd stick around for about as long it took for them to realize we weren't there. The good news is, we were able to give the police a description."

"I just hope it's enough. I've got a feeling that if those men get their hands on me again, they're not going to play as nice as they did last night."

"I've got a feeling you're right. Which brings us full circle. We've got to find a safe place to stay until we figure out who these guys are and what they really want."

"I think they made it pretty clear what they wanted. A disk that I don't have. I don't even know if it exists."

"Let's assume it does. You're sure Cody couldn't have slipped it in with your things?"

"I'm sure." She'd packed one suitcase and walked out. Cody hadn't even had time to realize she was going.

"So, it's somewhere else. We just need to figure out where, but first we've got to decide where we're going to stay."

"My parents' place—"

"Is exactly where they think you'll head. We need to go somewhere they won't expect. We could head back to New York. Stay at my place while—"

"Are you crazy? I'm not staying at your place."

"No need to sound so appalled by the idea," he said with a half smile that made her heart leap.

"I'm not appalled. I'm horrified. I don't even know you."

"You know me well enough to be sitting here talking to me, and that's all we'll be doing at my place. Unless you have other ideas."

"I do, and they don't include going to your place. My parents aren't the only people I know in Washington. I have an…" She let her voice trail off as Jackson shot a warning glance in the driver's direction. He didn't need to say what he was thinking. The driver hadn't bothered asking questions when they'd offered him a hundred dollars to wait at the back of the diner. He and Morgan could be criminals for all the driver knew, but it didn't seem to bother him. Would he think twice about relaying their conversation to someone for a price?

"We'll talk more on the plane," Jackson said, and Morgan nodded. Whether or not Helen would even open the door and allow her niece and a complete stranger to enter the sanctuary she'd carved for herself, Morgan couldn't say, but of all the places Morgan had ever been, Helen's was the closest she'd ever gotten to home. It would be good to stay there for a few days.

The taxi pulled up in front of the airport, and Jackson climbed out. Despite his relaxed demeanor, Morgan could feel the tightness in his muscles as he took her hand and helped her from the car. Were the men who'd followed them to the diner back here at the airport already?

Morgan wanted to hurry into the relative safety of the building, but her body wouldn't cooperate. She felt old and used up, her body aching with fatigue. No matter how much she wanted to run, she could only move slowly, rounding the cab as Jackson pulled her carry-on from the trunk, shuffling along as they moved away from the vehicle. Her ribs hurt with every breath. The pounding in her head and the pain in her jaw and cheek were becoming almost impossible to ignore.

What she wanted, what she needed, was a quiet place to rest and heal. A place shadowed by mountains, set deep in the evergreen forest of eastern Washington.

Not home, but close.

And maybe that was the most Morgan could ever hope for.

EIGHT

Waiting had never been something Morgan was good at, and she paced impatiently as the first-class passengers were called to board the flight to Spokane.

"Wearing a hole in the floor isn't going to get us on that plane any sooner," Jackson said, snagging the back of her jacket and pulling her to a stop.

She whirled to face him, ready to send him on his way like she should have the minute they'd returned to the airport. Fear had kept her silent. Fear and something else.

She met his eyes, tried to form the words that would make him turn and walk away, but they stuck in her throat, sealed there by her own weakness. She wanted to be strong. She wanted to be independent. She wanted, more than anything, to say she didn't need anyone and to mean it.

"It's going to be okay, Morgan. I promise." Jackson took her hand, his palm warming her chilled flesh. Auburn stubble darkened his jaw and there were shadows beneath his eyes. He looked as tired as she felt, but somehow managed to look stronger, more capable and more confident than she could ever hope to be.

Men like him should come with a warning label.

And an antidote.

One look in his eyes, one glance at his rugged face and she

was tempted to forget all the reasons why she shouldn't let herself trust him. Tempted to forget the hard lessons she'd learned from her marriage to Cody. Because as much as she wanted to believe Jackson was like her ex, she knew the truth. If there were heroes in the world, men who lived with integrity and honor, who championed the weak and protected the innocent, Jackson was one of them.

She shivered and took a step back, stopping short when Jackson didn't release her hand.

"You're cold," he said, slipping out of his sports coat.

"No, I'm fine." But he'd already settled the jacket around her shoulders. She could feel the heat of his body, could smell the faded scent of his cologne, and it made her long for things she was better off forgetting about.

"I can't take this, Jackson." She started to shrug out of the coat, but he grabbed the lapels and tugged it closed again.

"Sure you can."

"Keep handing me your jackets, and you won't have any left to wear," she said, half-heartedly attempting to shrug out of the jacket again. The fact was, she *was* cold, chilled to the bone with fear and fatigue.

"The one I lent you last night has already been returned, so you've got nothing to worry about." He buttoned the top button of the sports jacket, offered a quick smile that made Morgan's heart jump, and then nodded toward the line of passengers. "Looks like it's time to board. Ready?"

"As I'll ever be."

"You don't sound all that enthusiastic for someone who's going to visit family she hasn't seen in a few years."

"I'm…" She stopped herself before she said more than she should. Accepting Jackson's sports coat was one thing, telling all the reasons why she dreaded seeing her parents was something else entirely.

"What?"

"Just tired."

"And in pain?"

"That, too."

"So, let's get on the plane, and you can rest for a while." His hand rested on her waist as they joined the boarding passengers.

Morgan didn't bother to move away. What would be the point?

They were going to spend the next couple hours sitting knee to knee and shoulder to shoulder, and there wasn't much she could do about it.

Except tell him to go back to Lakeview.

She frowned as they boarded the flight and made their way through the half-empty cabin to their seats. She *should* tell him to go back. So why wasn't she?

"Looks like there won't be any problem sitting together this time," Jackson said, taking the seat beside Morgan.

"There wasn't any problem last time."

"Not after I gave up my seat in first class."

"I wondered if you had."

"It was that or sit near a group of executives who were discussing the pros and cons of on-site employee training."

"That might have been informative."

"But not nearly as interesting as sitting with you."

"No need for flattery, you've already gotten your way."

"What way?"

"You're heading to Spokane with me. I was planning on losing you in Chicago."

He chuckled, the sound deep and warm, inviting Morgan to join in.

She might have if she weren't so worried about what that would mean.

"So, where are we headed? You said you had an idea for a safe place." Jackson interrupted Morgan's thoughts.

"My Aunt Helen's place."

"I'm not sure that will be any safer than your parents'."

"That's because you don't know my aunt. She's got a cabin in the mountains. She goes to town once a week for supplies, but other than that, she rarely leaves the place."

"She's a hermit?"

"A potter. A renowned one, so she likes to keep her address private. She sells pieces of her work to galleries in Seattle, L.A. and New York, and she doesn't like to be disturbed when she's working."

"She sounds interesting."

"I guess so, but to a teenager who wanted to spend summers partying with friends, she was just…weird."

Jackson smiled at that, flashing dimples that had probably won him more than his fair share of hearts. "Your family spent a lot of time at her cabin?"

"*I* spent four summers at her cabin. The day school let out, my parents drove me there, dropped me off and left me. They'd come back to pick me up a couple days before school began." Four summers spent in the mountain cabin. No television. No contact with friends. Nothing but towering pine trees and the feel of clay beneath her fingers, smooth and cool and malleable. She hadn't been able to control her circumstances, but she *could* control the shape of the vases and bowls she threw.

"I guess there was a reason for that?"

"I was a troubled kid with a knack for causing chaos and drama. My parents' home was quiet and well structured until I showed up."

"Showed up? You make it sound like you arrived on their doorstep unannounced," Jackson said.

"Not quite, but close enough. We'd met twice before they adopted me. I don't think they had any idea what they were getting themselves into."

"I didn't realize you were adopted."

"Why would you?"

"I'd tell you, but I doubt you'd like what I had to say."

"Which, of course, means I've got to hear it, so, spill."

"When Jude moved to Virginia, he asked me to do some investigating. He had a list of people he thought might be responsible for the hit-and-run accident that nearly killed him. Your name was on the list."

"Because he helped put Cody in jail?"

"Exactly."

"I'm not sure I'm comfortable with the idea of you digging into my life."

"I was investigating your relationship to Jude. I didn't research your past. Which is why I didn't know you were adopted," Jackson responded. "Of course, now that we're discussing your past—"

"We're not."

"Sure we are, and I've got to admit, I'm curious. Were you in foster care?"

"I was in an orphanage in Latvia. My birth mother abandoned me when I was nine. I met the Alexandrias about a year later. They made two visits to the orphanage, and brought me home on the second trip."

"And?"

"That's it. The whole story. Or, as much of the story as I'm willing to share."

"You know why I became a private investigator, Morgan?"

"Because you're nosy and needed an excuse to dig into other people's business?"

He laughed and shook his head. "Maybe, but it was mostly because I'm good at getting answers."

"What happened in my past isn't something you need to find answers for, Jackson."

"No? It seems like your past has everything to do with the present, and that finding out about it will help us figure out what is going on."

"*Cody* has everything to do with the present, but he and I met in college. That's about as far back as any investigating needs to go."

She thought he would argue, but he nodded instead. "Fair enough. Everyone has secrets they've got a right to keep."

"Even you?" she asked and wished the question back immediately. Jackson's secrets were no more her business than hers were his.

"I'm not sure how secret they are, but I've got things I keep private."

"Like the reason you left your job as a homicide detective? It seems to me, a guy who's good at finding answers would excel at a job like that," Morgan said, desperate to steer the conversation away from herself, but not sure why she was steering it toward Jackson.

Not sure?

Of course she was sure. She was curious. It was as plain and simple as that.

Which made it really complicated.

"Forget I said that. It's really none of my business."

"I don't mind answering," he responded and short of lying and saying she had no interest in hearing his answer, Morgan could do nothing but listen. "After my sister Lindsey died, I lost my objectivity. Without it, I couldn't do my job effectively."

"That must have been tough."

"It was. Lindsey was murdered by her estranged husband. He beat her, strangled her and left her for dead. She died in the hospital three days after the attack. After that, every time a woman was killed, I thought of my sister. Each crime scene was like a testimony to her death, and each one seemed to point to a husband or boyfriend's guilt. Even when it didn't." His voice was tight and hard, his hands fisted, and Morgan reached out and touched his knuckles, let her palm rest against his warm skin.

"I'm so, so sorry, Jackson," she said, knowing the words weren't enough. Could never be enough.

"You said that before," he responded, turning his hand beneath hers, so that they were palm to palm, finger to finger.

"I know it doesn't help." She should move her hand away.

She should, but didn't. Just let him curl his fingers around hers, squeeze gently. "It doesn't change anything, but it does help. I'm going to call Sheriff Reed while we wait for take-off. The police have had plenty of time to find our guys and bring them in for questioning."

He released her hand, and she pulled it back into her lap. Told herself she couldn't still feel the warmth of his touch, the gentle pressure of his fingers curling around hers.

It only took Jackson a few minutes to finish his conversation. He was frowning as he shoved his cell phone back into his pocket.

"Bad news?" Morgan asked.

"Good and bad. The police are still searching for our guys. They've staked out the airport. No sign of two men fitting the description we gave boarding a flight to Spokane. Seeing as how this is the only flight to Spokane, I consider that good news."

"So what's the bad news?"

"Both men are still on the loose, and we're no closer to finding the answers we need to keep you safe."

"Has Sheriff Reed been able to find out any more information about Cody's death?"

"He didn't say, and I didn't ask. We'll call again when we land in Spokane. I want to do a search on Cody's business and on his clients. Sheriff Reed might have some of that information."

"If he doesn't, Cody's parents might. They cleaned out his

office and our home after he was convicted and sentenced. I think they took all his things to storage."

"Would they be willing to let you look through it? Or to search through it themselves?"

"They haven't spoken to me since Cody was arrested. I doubt they're going to open up now."

"Even if talking to you means finding the person who murdered their son?"

"Maybe. But you still may have better luck calling them yourself. During the trial they were happy to be interviewed by the press and to answer any questions the police and attorneys posed." They'd also been more than happy to paint Morgan in a negative light. Their goal had been to see their son acquitted. They didn't care how many lies they told to do it.

"I think I remember seeing them on the news during Cody's trial. His mother cried with dry eyes," Jackson responded.

"Lila Bradshaw didn't believe in crying. It smeared even the most waterproof mascara. At least, that's what she told me a few hours before I married Cody."

"She sounds like good mother material," Jackson said wryly, and Morgan nodded her agreement.

"She didn't have a maternal bone in her body. She loved Cody, but I always thought that had more to do with his success than the fact that he was her son."

"But she wasn't nearly as fond of you and your success?"

"Making pottery doesn't equate to making money. In Lila's eyes, it was a waste of time, energy and resources."

"That's too bad."

"It was, but I didn't let it bother me." Much.

Jackson eyed her for a moment, as if he sensed the lie in her words. She refused to look away or to admit what they both knew was the truth. "Do you have their phone number?"

"Unless they've changed it."

"I'll give them a call tomorrow. See what I can find out."

"If you're thinking Lila will search through Cody's things for you, I don't think it's going to happen. She's never been the kind to do anything unless it benefited her."

"I'm more interested in finding out whether or not anyone else has been calling and asking them questions. I'd also like to know if she's had a break-in recently."

"You think someone already searched through Cody's things?"

"Whoever is looking for that disk probably searched every other avenue before approaching Cody."

"It's been almost two years since he went to jail, so I guess that would fit."

"It fits. That doesn't mean it's right. We'll have to wait to see what Sheriff Reed finds out. Put the information together. See if we can get the true story."

Morgan nodded, fatigue and pain sapping what little energy she had. There were so many unknowns. Too many. When she'd met Cody, she'd imagined him to be all her dreams wrapped up in one package. Love, marriage, family, a place to belong. She'd been wrong, but she'd learned a lot from her relationship with Cody. She'd learned that wanting something couldn't make it happen, and she'd learned that trying hard didn't always mean being successful.

And she'd learned that she could live life alone and be content to do it.

They were good lessons. Sometimes she thought they were God lessons, things He was determined to teach her so that she could grow. Other times she just thought they were a product of living thirty years.

The plane taxied onto the runway, picking up speed and lifting into the air, putting more distance between Morgan and the dream she'd built in Lakeview. Bringing her closer to the family that had never felt like hers and a past she'd only partially made peace with.

NINE

The plane landed a little after midnight, and Jackson waited until the other passengers began departing before he gently touched Morgan. She didn't stir.

"Morgan?" he said, touching her shoulder again.

This time, she jerked upright, a half-formed scream dying on her lips as she met his eyes.

"Sorry about that. I didn't mean to scare you."

"You didn't. Much," she said, trying a smile that ended with a grimace. Her skin was parchment white, her bruises deep blue and black, and the fear in her eyes made Jackson want to pull her against his chest, brush the silky hair from her cheeks and promise her again that everything would be all right. "I guess it's time to get off this plane."

"Your parents will be worried if we don't appear eventually."

"Actually, I told them not to bother meeting me."

"I see," Jackson said, grabbing Morgan's carry-on from the overhead compartment.

"See what?"

"You and your family don't get along."

"Sure we do."

"Then why didn't you want them to meet you at the airport?"

"They live twenty miles from here, and I planned to rent a

car. It's for the best now, anyway, since I won't be staying with them." She shrugged, not defensive, but not entirely comfortable with his comment. He must have hit a nerve.

"Why don't you call your aunt now and let her know we're coming?" Jackson suggested, scanning the small airport. It was nearly midnight and the place was almost empty. He should have found that reassuring. Instead, he felt exposed. A target with a giant bull's-eye attached to his back.

He frowned, putting a hand on Morgan's arm and holding her in place. "Where's the car rental place?"

"At the end of this corridor. Unless they've moved it. I haven't been back here in two years, so that's a possibility."

"Let's hope it's still there. The sooner we get out of here, the happier I'll be."

"You think they're here?" she whispered, her muscles tense beneath his hand.

"Not the guys we saw in Chicago, but maybe one of their friends."

"You're acting like I've got an army chasing after me."

"I don't know how many people might be coming after you, but I'm not willing to take chances."

"Sheriff Reed said the local police know I'm coming. Maybe they've staked out the airport."

"Maybe." Probably, but Jackson still wasn't comfortable, the eerie feeling of being watched urging him to hurry.

"There she is," a deep voice bellowed from behind them, and Jackson pivoted sharply, stepping between Morgan and whatever threat was coming.

A dark-haired man jogged toward them, several people trailing along behind. Six foot two. Maybe two hundred pounds. A broad smile doing little to ease the hard edges of his deeply tanned face, the guy looked military and he looked dangerous.

Jackson tensed, his hand reaching for the gun he always

carried, finding it gone. Left back in Lakeview so he could fly to Spokane with Morgan.

"Little sis, you'd better stop hiding behind your beau, because I'd hate to have to shove him out of the way to get my hug," the man called out, and Morgan stepped out from behind Jackson.

"Benjamin! What are you doing here?" she cried, throwing herself into the man's arms.

"Dad called to tell me what happened. I drove over from Seattle earlier today. Let me see you." Benjamin eased away from Morgan's hold, his gaze jumping from her bruised face to Jackson. "I guess you've got some explanation for how you let this happen."

"Her ex-husband was a loser," Jackson responded, not taking offense at Benjamin's tone. He'd always been just as protective of his sisters, and he didn't see any need to correct the assumption that he was Morgan's boyfriend and somehow could have prevented the attack.

"And Jackson isn't my beau, as you so quaintly put it. He's my…" Morgan glanced at Jackson. "He saved my life and wanted to make sure I arrived here in one piece."

"Thank goodness we caught you. I was worried we'd missed you and you were on your way to the house." A silver-haired woman stepped around Benjamin. Pretty and slim with deep brown eyes and a gentle smile, she eyed Morgan with concern. "It's worse than you said, honey. Why didn't you tell us how hurt you were? Dad would have come to Lakeview."

"Bruises always look worse than they are, Mom," Morgan responded, hugging her mother. "I told Dad you shouldn't bother coming."

"Bother? What bother? You're our little girl," a tall, thin man said, patting Morgan gently on the back before turning to greet Jackson.

"I'm Richard Alexandria. This is my wife, Sue, and my

youngest daughter, Lauren." He gestured to the silver-haired woman and a tall, lanky teen.

"Jackson Sharo. Nice to meet you all."

"We can't thank you enough for what you've done for our daughter."

"No thanks are necessary."

"Of course they are. You saved Morgan's life, *and* you escorted her all the way across the country," the teen said, eyeing Jackson with curiosity. "Mom and Dad have been worried sick since Morgan called. The only reason Dad didn't get on a plane and fly to Virginia is because Morgan is so pigheaded—"

"That's enough, Lauren. I'm sure that Jackson doesn't want to hear Dad's opinion of me," Morgan cut in. "Now, come give your big sis a hug. It's been too long since we've seen each other."

"Two years too long," Lauren said, stepping into Morgan's open arms. The two couldn't be more different. Blonde and brunette. Pale and tan. Tall and short. Green eyes and blue eyes. Despite the differences, it was obvious they loved each other. Watching them made Jackson long for what he'd been avoiding for too long. When he got back to New York, he'd call his folks, arrange to spend a weekend with them.

"Why don't we get this show on the road? I think Morgan needs to be tucked into bed with a few ice packs," Benjamin said, and Jackson watched as Morgan took a step back from her sister, straightened her shoulders and brushed strands of hair from her bruised cheek.

"About that, Jackson thinks it might be better if I stay somewhere other than the ranch."

"He's wrong," Benjamin responded, frowning in Jackson's direction.

"If I am, it won't be the first time. But the men who attacked Morgan are still at large. It will be easy enough for them to find her at your parents' place."

"No more easy than it will be to find her anywhere else. I say—"

"Actually, he's got a point, Ben," Richard cut in. "Morgan needs to go somewhere where she won't be found. And, if I know my daughter, she's already thought of the perfect place. Probably a place where she spent a few summers when she was a teen. Am I right, Morgan?"

"Yes, it's probably the best place for now. Aunt Helen is so far from civilization, it will be difficult for anyone to find her."

"I'm sure you're right, honey, but I was so looking forward to spending time with you," Sue said, hugging her daughter again.

"I was looking forward to spending time with you, too," Morgan responded, and Jackson wondered if it was true. Despite the hugs and smiles she'd offered, Morgan seemed ill at ease and tense, as if she were more a stranger than someone who belonged.

Had it always been that way?

Or was she simply worried about the danger she was in, exhausted by what she'd been through and too tired to show the kind of enthusiasm for the family reunion that everyone else seemed to have?

"Why don't we all drive over to Helen's together? We can make sure Morgan gets settled in, and save Jackson the effort of riding out to Aunt Helen's house with her." Benjamin seemed determined to keep his sister close, and Jackson respected him for that. That didn't mean he was going to turn tail and run. He'd started a job that he planned to finish. No matter how much Morgan's brother might want him to walk away.

"The reason I got a rental car was so that I wouldn't have to bother—" Morgan explained.

"Please, don't say you're bothering us. You're our daughter. It is never a bother to help you out," Richard said, the sharpness in his tone unmistakable.

"I know that, Dad, but…" She shook her head, and Jackson was sure there were tears in her eyes. Surprised, he stepped close and dropped a hand on her shoulder.

"It's better if the four of you head back to your place. If someone is staking out the airport—"

"Do you think that's a possibility?" Benjamin cut in, and Jackson nodded.

"The guys who attacked Morgan were at the Chicago airport. The police put out an APB, but as far as I know, they haven't been caught yet. Even if they have, there's no reason to think they're the only two people coming after your sister."

"Meaning?"

"Cody worked for a lot of high-powered, wealthy clients. If one of them is responsible for what happened to Morgan, there's no telling what kind of manpower he has at his disposal."

"Hired thugs don't come cheap, but someone with money may not be worried about the expense," Benjamin muttered, and Jackson nodded again.

"Exactly."

"That's assuming the guys who came after me were hired thugs. It's possible they're the ones who want the disk. Maybe they were friends of Cody's."

"Disk?" Richard asked.

"It's a long story. Mind if I tell it tomorrow? I'm beat."

"Of course you are!" Sue wrapped an arm around Morgan's waist. "You've been through something terrible. I'm so glad you're all right, sweetie. I've been so worried since you called."

"I didn't mean to give you more to worry about."

"Are you kidding me?" Lauren asked. "Mom and Dad love to worry. They excel at it, even. Personally, much as I hate what happened to you, I'm glad you're here. Gives the parents something to focus on besides my bad grades," Lauren said with a grin, and Morgan laughed.

"You haven't changed much, Lauren."

"You have. You're quieter. Or maybe it's just because you're hurt."

"Yeah. Maybe." Morgan took her sister's hand, her mother's arm still wrapped around her waist. They made a pretty picture, the three Alexandria women, but the more Jackson looked the more he saw what he had seen before. Morgan's discomfort. The tight, tense way she held herself just slightly away from the other two women.

"Does Helen know you're coming?" Richard asked as the group walked to the rental-car booth.

"No. I thought I was going to stay with you, until we realized we'd been followed."

"Would you like me to call her for you? You know how Helen is about unexpected visitors," Sue offered.

"I don't mind calling her. The number is the same, right?"

"You'd know, if you ever bothered to call her. Last time I was over at her place, Aunt Helen said she hadn't heard from you in months."

"That's because every time we talk, we argue."

"About that jerk Cody and why you wasted your youth with him?"

"Lauren! You shouldn't speak ill of the dead."

"What? Dying makes the guy something better than a slug?"

"Lauren Elizabeth Alexandria, you apologize to your sister this instant."

"For what? She knows he was a slug. Right?"

"Better than anyone, but Mom is right. You shouldn't speak ill of the dead."

"Why is it that adults always stick together. Even when they're wrong?" The teen continued to prattle on about the unfairness of life as Morgan signed the paperwork and took the keys to the rental car.

"That's it. We're ready to head out," she said, cutting off her sister's rambling diatribe.

"Did you bring luggage? I can get it for you if you did."

"Thanks, Ben, but the carry-on is it."

"Will that be enough? I've got some of your old clothes packed away," Sue offered. "If you need more, I can bring them to Helen's for you."

"Her place is an hour drive from yours. I wouldn't want to be a bo—"

"Wouldn't go there if I were you," Jackson whispered into Morgan's ear, cutting off the word he knew she was going to say. The word she'd used over and over again during the time she'd been speaking to her parents.

"Right. Thanks." She smiled, looking into Jackson's eyes for the first time since they'd left the plane. The black-and-green bruises on her cheek now covered the entire left side of her face and were inching up toward the outer corner of her eye. Somehow, she still managed to look lovely, her eyes pure icy-blue surrounded by thick black lashes. Usually, Jackson preferred statuesque blondes to short brunettes, but there was something about Morgan that made him want to look and keep looking. Something that drew his eye again and again.

It wasn't the bruises.

Wasn't the eyes.

It was her.

Jackson shouldn't be intrigued. Morgan was no different than any other client he'd worked with, and he needed to treat her with the same respectful distance he'd cultivated during his time on the force and his years working as a detective.

Needed to, but was having trouble doing it.

He frowned, walking with the family as they made their way through the airport. The last thing he wanted was to get involved more deeply in Morgan's life than he already was. Protecting her, helping her find the disk Cody had hidden, those were things he was willing to do. Noticing how beautiful she looked, that was something entirely different.

Yet he'd found himself noticing again and again.

He wasn't sure how he felt about it, but for now he had plenty of other things to worry about. Once he got Morgan settled at her aunt's house, he was going to plug into the Internet and start digging for answers. Someone somewhere knew what had gotten Cody Bradshaw killed. Jackson planned to find out who, he planned to find out what and then he planned to go back to New York and his job.

It's what he planned, but he'd learned a long time ago that plans didn't always work out the way they were meant to. God had a sense of humor. That's what Lindsey used to say. Maybe she was right. Maybe He did. Jackson wasn't one to spend much time thinking about God one way or another. Though lately he'd found himself wondering if he should. Life was finite. It had a beginning and an end. He'd spent the first thirty-two years of his life pursuing his career and his passions. If he had only one year left, one month, one week, would he spend it the same way?

Probably not.

Lindsey's death had been devastating, but it had opened Jackson's eyes. Let him see the truth about the life he'd chosen. What it hadn't done was to show him a better, more fulfilling way to live.

Then again, maybe that wasn't something that could be found. Maybe it was something that had to be learned. One day at a time. One experience at a time.

Double doors led out into a parking garage, where the rental car was located. Jackson pushed the doors open, and stepped outside, inhaling clean, cold air and the subtle scent of exhaust as he surveyed the silent garage.

"Everything look okay?" Benjamin stepped out behind him, and Jackson nodded.

"For now."

"Then let's move out while we've got the opportunity. You guys ready?" he called out to his family, and they moved into the garage. Richard, Sue and Lauren close together. Morgan just a little apart.

And despite everything he'd been telling himself about keeping his distance, Jackson moved close, offering her the connection she didn't seem to have with her family. She glanced up, met his eyes and smiled a smile that Jackson didn't think he'd ever get tired of seeing.

For some reason that didn't worry him nearly as much as he thought it should.

TEN

Morgan hated goodbyes. The long, drawn-out hugs, the easy promises about keeping in touch, they were things she liked to avoid. Unfortunately, they were things the rest of her family seemed to love.

She wasn't wearing a watch, but she was sure if she checked the clock on her cell phone, she'd see that she'd been standing next to the rental car, saying goodbye to her family for the better part of fifteen minutes.

"Are you sure you don't want me to drive some clothes over to Helen's tonight? I'm sure there are things at the house that will fit you," her mother said for what must have been the tenth time. Morgan wasn't sure whether she felt more touched or frustrated.

"I've got enough clothes in the carry-on for a couple of days."

"I'll bring some tomorrow then."

"That's fine."

"And I'll bring you the huckleberry pie I made this afternoon."

"You made huckleberry pie?"

"It's still your favorite, isn't it?"

"It has been since the day you brought me home and fed it to me with dinner."

"You still remember that?"

"How could I forget? After everyone went to bed, I snuck downstairs and ate two more pieces."

"That was you? I thought for sure your brothers had been at it."

"It was me," Morgan said, smiling a little with the memory. Pain shot through her jaw and lip, raced up her cheekbone and lodged in her temple, reminding her of just how anxious she was to take some of the heavy-duty painkillers the doctor had prescribed, then climb into bed and pull the covers over her head.

"Then I'm glad I decided to bake today. It's like a second homecoming. How about I come around noon—"

"Mrs. Alexandria, I know Morgan appreciates the offer, but we can't take any chances that someone will follow you. It may be best if I bring Morgan to your house."

"Call me Sue. And, I hadn't thought about the possibility of being followed. I certainly don't want to put Morgan in any more danger."

"How about we call you, Mom? First thing in the morning, we'll discuss it. Okay?" Morgan tried to end the conversation, but doubted it would work. Her parents were two of the most compassionate, loving people she knew. When someone they loved was hurting, they wanted more than anything to take the pain away.

Unfortunately, in Morgan's case, that was an impossibility.

"Tomorrow is Sunday," her father said. "How about we all just meet at the church? We can have brunch afterward, and then you can go back to Helen's place?" He made the suggestion as if he really expected Morgan to go to church with green-and-black bruises all over her face.

"I can't go to church looking like this," she responded, gesturing to the painful bruises.

"Why not?"

"Because people will stare."

"And they didn't stare when you were fifteen and decided to give yourself a Mohawk?"

"That was different."

"How so?"

"I was young and too stupid to want anonymity."

"No one is going to care if you've got a few bruises," Lauren interjected. "Peggy Harrison had a face-lift two weeks ago and showed up at church a few days later, her skin all bruised and puffy looking. If she can show up looking like that, you can show up looking like you do."

"Lauren!"

"What? It's only the truth, Mom, and you know it."

"Knowing it and saying it are two different things."

"Well, I'm just trying to get my sis to come to church with me. There's nothing wrong with that, is there?"

"We'll discuss it at home."

"But you are coming. Right, Morgan?" Lauren asked, her eyes so filled with hope and enthusiasm, Morgan didn't have the heart to say no.

"Sure. Just for the service, though. Sunday school starts way too early for me. I'll see you then," she said, opening the car door and hoping her family would get the hint.

"We'll see you then, sweetie." Her father leaned forward and kissed her cheek, then stepped back. "I think we'd better head back home and let Morgan and Jackson be on their way."

Another quick burst of goodbyes and Morgan's family was off, heading across the parking lot, their voices echoing through the space as Morgan watched them go.

"Ready to get out of here?" Jackson asked after the sound of their departure had faded, his eyes filled with amusement and a warmth that seemed to spear straight into Morgan's heart. She looked away, not wanting him to see what she was feeling.

"I've been ready for fifteen minutes. Thanks for everything you've done, but I think I'll be okay on my own now."

"You're exhausted. So am I. Let's not waste time fighting an argument that I'm going to win." He sounded as weary as Morgan felt, and he was right. They'd been traveling for most of the day, had been up for most of the previous night. The time for arguing was long past. He was here, and she wasn't even sure she wanted to try to send him away.

"Maybe you should drive."

"You're giving in pretty easily," he said, taking the key she offered.

"Like you said, we're both exhausted. I don't have the energy to do anything but get in the car and go." She climbed into the passenger seat, her body heavy with fatigue, her mind numb. She needed to call Helen and let her know they were coming. She wasn't sure what her aunt's reaction would be. They hadn't parted on the best of terms, and things hadn't gotten any better in the years since Morgan's marriage.

"Where are we headed?" Jackson asked as he started the engine.

"Golden Apple. It's about eighty miles from here. My aunt is two miles down a dirt road just outside of town."

"You know the address?"

"Sure."

"There's a GPS unit. Want to input it?"

Morgan fumbled to do as Jackson suggested, her fingers shaking as she punched in the information. Fear, adrenaline, anxiety, relief. She wasn't sure which she felt more. Once she finally managed to input the address, she pulled her cell phone out and dialed Helen's number.

"Hello?" Morgan's aunt answered on the third ring, and Morgan tensed, unsure of her reception. It wasn't that Helen had ever been unkind, but the silences between them when they'd attempted to talk had always seemed filled with Helen's disapproval of Morgan's decision to marry Cody.

She'd been right to disapprove. That was obvious now, but the silence was still there, and Morgan had no idea how to break it.

"Hi, Aunt Helen. It's Morgan."

"Morgan! Your mom said there's been some kind of trouble and that you were coming to town. Are you okay? What happened?"

"Cody… It's hard to explain. Listen, I hate to ask, but I need a place to stay for a while."

"You're not staying with your parents?"

"There are some people after me. The first place they'll look is Mom and Dad's."

"Then you're welcome here. You know my door is always open to you."

"I appreciate it."

"When will you be here? I'll need to make up the guest bed."

"An hour and a half. And I'm not alone. I've got a…" *Friend* didn't seem the right word. *Man* was too general. "…private detective with me. He's going to do some research on Cody. See if he can figure out what's going on."

"I see. He'll have to sleep on the pullout couch in the den."

"I'm sure he won't mind," she said, glancing at Jackson, who'd followed the GPS directions onto I-90.

"Mind what?"

"Sleeping on my aunt's pullout couch."

"I've slept on worse."

"He says he's fine with it, Aunt Helen."

"I'll get it ready. Are you hungry? I can make you something to eat."

"I'm too tired to know how I feel." Except for the fact that she was in pain, but Morgan decided not to mention that.

"I'll put together something. If you're hungry when you get here, you can eat it. If you're not, it'll keep until tomorrow."

"Thanks, Aunt Helen."

"You don't have to thank me, sweetie. We're family." Helen hung up, and Morgan shoved the phone back in her purse.

Family.

The word seemed to hang in the air, whisper into Morgan's heart. Family and home were two things she'd wanted more than anything, but they were the two things she wasn't sure she'd ever really have. It wasn't that she didn't believe what Helen was saying. It wasn't even that she didn't believe they really were family, but there was something missing. Two things. A brother and sister who had been ripped from Morgan's life. Maybe she should have been able to forget them, to move on and to embrace the new family she'd been given. But she hadn't, and that made it so much more difficult to accept the love the Alexandrias offered.

"You're quiet," Jackson said, and Morgan could hear the questions in his voice.

"Just thinking."

"About?"

"Family."

"You've got a good one."

"I know."

"So why are you so uncomfortable around them?"

"I'm not."

"Sure you are. They laugh and talk and you hang back. Like you're not really a part of any of it."

"I'm exhausted, and my family's enthusiasm can be overwhelming."

"My family is the same way. They mean well, though."

"I know, and most of the time I enjoy it. Noise is a lot more comforting than silence. When I was a kid…" Her voice trailed off, and she pressed her lips together. Talking about her life in Latvia wasn't something she made a habit of doing.

"What?"

"Nothing."

"You're just going to leave me hanging?"

"Yes."

"Too bad. We've got another fifty miles to go, and I'm tired. A good story might help me keep my eyes open."

"Are you playing the sympathy card?"

"It was that or the I-saved-your-life card, and I didn't think you'd go for that one." He shot a grin in her direction, but the darkness couldn't hide the deep shadows beneath his eyes or the lines of fatigue that bracketed his mouth. She wanted to smooth them from his face, let her fingers slide over his stubbled jaw.

And that terrified her.

She clenched her fists to keep from doing what she shouldn't and focused on the road, the review mirror, the trees that flew by outside the window. Anything but Jackson.

"So, how about it? Want to share in the interest of keeping me awake and us safe?"

No, but she'd do it in the interest of keeping her mind off things she shouldn't be dwelling on. Like how nice it was to be making the trip to Aunt Helen's with someone else, or how being with Jackson felt comfortable and exciting all at the same time.

"It's not that interesting of a tale, but if you're that bent on hearing it—"

"I am."

"When I was a kid, we lived in an apartment in Latvia."

"We?"

"My sister, brother and mother. It was a small place. I remember one big room with a kitchen and a closet and a small bathroom with a tub. My sister and brother and I slept on the floor. My mother slept on the couch when she was home. There wasn't much to eat, and there weren't a lot of blankets. I can remember being very hungry and very cold."

"You had a tough time."

"I had the two people that meant the most in the world to me. Katia and Nikolai. When my mother was gone, we were typical kids. Loud and silly and always looking for trouble, but when my mother came home, we were as quiet as mice. I can remember Nikolai saying when Mother came home drunk, *shh, little sisters, be as quiet as mice.*"

"He was older than you?"

"By five years. He used to make sure we had food to eat and clean clothes to wear."

"What happened to him?" Jackson asked, the question stabbing another hole in Morgan's heart. She didn't know what had happened. Didn't know if Nikolai was alive or dead, happy or sad. After a decade of searching fruitlessly for Katia and Nikolai, she'd given up hope that she'd ever find out.

"I don't know. Our little sister was adopted by an American couple. I remember the day they came for her. She was shrieking as the orphanage director carried her away. A month later, the Alexandrias came to meet me. That was the last time I saw Nikolai."

"He was fifteen?"

"About that."

"I'll help you find him and your sister."

Say no thank you. Tell him you don't want help.

That's what she knew she should do, but it wasn't what she wanted to do. Jackson was a private detective. If there was even a slim possibility that he could help her find Nikolai and Katia, could she really tell him not to?

There was more to it than that.

There was a sense Morgan had that if anyone could find her siblings, it would be Jackson. That somehow she could trust him to *want* to find them as much as she did and that she could count on him to search as hard as she had.

Trust him? Count on him?

"I spent a decade trying to find them, Jackson. I'm not sure there's any stone left unturned."

"It can't hurt to look." He was right, of course, and no matter how afraid she was that she was getting in too deep, Morgan had to let him try.

"I guess it can't. How much do you charge?"

"Nothing."

"You don't work for free."

"Who said anything about working? I just said I'd try to find them for you." He glanced in the review mirror again and frowned.

"What's wrong?"

"There's a car coming up behind us."

"You think we should be worried about it?"

"Probably not, but I'm keeping my eye on things. This is a rural area. I can't imagine there'll be a whole lot of traffic at this time of night."

Morgan shifted in her seat and looked out the back window. In the distance, headlights cut through the darkness. Jackson was probably right. It was probably nothing, but fear shivered along her spine and her pulse picked up speed. "Do you think there's any way we were followed from the airport?"

"I wish I could say I didn't, but I'm not sure. Cody's clients had money at their disposal. It's possible someone was waiting at the airport for us to arrive."

"Maybe you can get his parents to give you access to his work files," Morgan said. "If we had a list of his clients, we might be able to pare it down enough to find the person responsible for his death."

"I'll call them tomorrow, and if they refuse to help, they may change their tune for the police."

"I'm sure they will. The Bradshaws have always been completely cooperative with the police."

"What about the business partner?"

"Sean?"

"Yeah. Would he have had an account log?"

"Probably."

"Any idea what happened to it?"

"I imagine everything of Sean's was given to his parents."

"He wasn't married?"

"No. I don't think he was even dating anyone when he was…when he died."

"Do you know his parents?" Jackson asked, his voice tight, his gaze jumping to the rearview mirror again.

Was the car getting closer?

Morgan glanced out the back window.

It seemed like the headlights were closer, but maybe that was just her imagination working overtime. "I never met Sean's parents. I think they lived in New York, but I'm not even sure of that."

"We'll find out. See if we can get any information from them, but first let's lose the car behind us."

"You think they're following us."

"I think I'm not going to take any chances." He turned off the headlights, plunging the road into darkness.

"What are you doing? We're going to drive off the road!"

"That's exactly what I'm planning. There's a dirt road up ahead on the right. We'll take that, turn off the engine and pray whoever is behind us goes right by."

"How can you see the road? It's black as pitch out here."

"I can see just fine." As if to prove his point, he turned sharply, bouncing onto what could only be the dirt road. Something scraped against the window near Morgan's ear, and she jumped, barely managing to hold back a scream.

"Relax. It's just a tree." Jackson patted her knee, the heat of his touch spreading through her, but doing nothing to ease her icy fear.

Jackson cut the engine, plunging them into darkness so complete Morgan could feel it pressing in on her, stealing her breath and her thoughts. Darkness had never been her friend. Not when she'd been a scared kid, not when she'd been a rebellious teen and certainly not now.

She took a deep, steadying breath, trying to slow her racing pulse. She was a thirty-year-old woman, and she needed to get control of herself. There was nothing to fear.

Not yet.

But if the person in the approaching vehicle really was following them, there would be.

She tensed as the quiet chug of a car engine broke the silence, faint but growing louder. It could be anyone, but Morgan's thundering heart was shouting that it was danger. She wanted to shove the door open, race out into the night, find a place to hide.

Jackson's hand slipped around hers, and he squeezed gently. "Everything is going to be okay."

"You can't know that."

"No, but I'm choosing to believe it."

He squeezed her hand again, and Morgan didn't even try to pull away. Just sat still and silent as the car drew closer, its headlights illuminating the road. Was the driver looking for them? Would he see their car parked off the road?

Please, God, I just need a little more time.

To spend with the people she loved, to find those she was missing, to be a better person than she'd been during her marriage to Cody.

The prayer filled her mind and her heart, and she imagined it pushing through the oppressive darkness, flying up to the feet of God, echoing the prayers and petitions of millions of other souls.

Did God hear?

Did He care?

Morgan didn't know.

Maybe she didn't need to.

Maybe, like Jackson, she must simply choose to believe.

ELEVEN

Morgan's hand was cool and dry, her body stiff with fear as the car approached. Jackson slid his arm around her waist, pulling her close. He could feel her tension, hear the harsh rasping of her breath as the headlights drew closer.

"Relax," he murmured, his lips brushing the soft hair near her ear. He could imagine doing the same in other circumstances. Imagine allowing himself to inhale the sweet, berry scent of her shampoo, run his fingers beneath the hair at her nape, feel the warmth of the skin there.

That worried him.

He was crossing a line he'd never crossed before. Not when he'd worked as a beat cop, not when he'd worked homicide and definitely not while he'd been working for Kane. Business was business, and he didn't believe in mixing it with anything else. He'd seen too many men and women go down that path. Usually with disastrous results.

Yet he was sitting in a dark car, holding Morgan and imagining different circumstances, other moments with her.

He frowned, tracking the approaching car as it slowly moved along the road, forcing himself to ignore the warm yielding weight of Morgan's shoulder as she pressed in close.

The car was coming too slowly.

It didn't seem to Jackson that the car was going more than twenty miles an hour. Way under the posted sixty-miles-an-hour speed limit.

It could mean nothing or it could mean that the driver was looking for something. Or someone.

"He's driving awfully slowly," Morgan whispered, as if somehow her words could carry outside the car and to the ears of whoever was driving the car.

"I was thinking the same."

"What are we going to do?"

"Wait."

"For how long?"

"Until he passes."

"He could pull over."

"He could."

"I guess you've got a plan if that happens."

Not a good one, but Jackson didn't think sharing that with Morgan was the best idea. "Let's just wait and see what happens."

"I've never been good at waiting."

"Looks like you won't have to be. He's already passed." Jackson leaned toward the window, trying to catch sight of the passing car's license plate. The foliage and distance prevented a clear view, and he pushed open the car door.

"What are you doing?" Morgan grabbed his hand.

"Going to see if I can get a look at the license plate."

"What if he sees you?"

"How will he? It's pitch-black, and he's looking ahead, not back." He eased his hand from hers and stepped out of the car. Chilly night air seeped through his jacket as he jogged to edge of the road and pressed close to a stand of tall, narrow ever-greens. If the driver looked back, all he'd see were trees.

Up ahead, the car was rounding a curve in the road, its headlights bouncing off a rocky outcrop that led to a steep incline. Even with a clear view of the vehicle, it was impossible for Jackson to read the license plate. He was too far away, and the letters and numbers were nothing more than a dark smudge.

Behind him, the car door opened and the pad of feet against dirt and grass filled the silence. He didn't turn, just waited as Morgan approached, feeling her presence before she spoke.

"Did you get it?"

"He was too far away."

"What now?"

"Now we get back in the car and drive to your aunt's house," he said, starting to turn away from the road, then freezing as headlights appeared near the outcrop of rocks, splashed onto the road and continued toward them.

He grabbed Morgan's hand, nearly yanking her off her feet as he raced back to the car. "Get in."

"Do you think—"

"Get in!" He gave her a gentle shove, then followed her into the car, slamming the door shut. "Duck down."

This time she didn't question him, just sank down low, her face a pale oval in the darkness. "Was it the same car?"

"I don't know," Jackson responded, peering up over the seat. He doubted the headlights would fall on their car, but he couldn't be sure. The approaching vehicle was coming from a different angle, and Jackson braced himself as the car's headlights illuminated the road a hundred yards from where they sat.

Was it the same car?

Maybe, but this time it came more quickly, flying past so rapidly, Jackson only had time to note the size and dark color. Both were similar to the vehicle that had passed a few minutes ago, but that didn't mean they were the same.

It also didn't mean they weren't.

This time, he didn't wait. As soon as the car was out of

sight, he started the engine of the rental and pulled back onto the main road.

"Do you think he'll come back?"

"I don't even know if it was the same car."

"I need to find that disk," Morgan muttered more to herself than to Jackson.

"We will."

"Whatever is on it, it's got to be something big."

"Or something not so big that has the potential to ruin someone."

"Like?"

"Tax fraud. It's not capital murder, but getting caught can sure ruin a life."

"Do you really think it's that simple?"

"I don't know, but it's a possibility. Maybe some of Cody's clients wanted to hold on to a little more of their earnings than they should have."

"What if they did? It doesn't seem like a crime worth committing murder to hide."

"I guess that depends on who you are and what you've got to lose."

"So, we need to figure out who Cody's clients were and then decide who had the most to lose?"

"It's a start."

"It's funny, I was married to him for six years, and I had no idea Cody was so corrupt. Or maybe it's not so funny. Maybe it's just sad."

"You're not the first spouse who's wanted to believe in her partner. I've worked for a lot of men and women who desperately want to believe that the person they married is the dream they fell in love with."

"The problem with dreams is they're always much better than reality."

"You think so?'

"You're asking a woman who was married to a man who murdered his business partner and lied about the reason why."

"I've been wanting to bring that up. I'm glad you did instead."

"What?"

"Cody's reasons for murdering Sean."

"He said the two of us were having an affair, and that the crime was one of passion. He lied."

"So you and Sean—"

"—Were good friends. Nothing more. As a matter of fact, the only time I saw Sean was when I visited the office or when Cody invited him over for dinner." Morgan sounded completely at ease with the discussion. In Jackson's experience, people who were lying were a lot more eager to change the subject than Morgan seemed.

"Why would Cody lie about something like that?"

"To save his hide. He probably thought he could get convicted of manslaughter rather than murder."

"That makes sense, but what it doesn't do is explain why Cody would murder his business partner. They were friends, right?"

"Since high school."

"And they went into business together right after college?"

"About a year later. Cody was working at a firm in Seattle, and Sean had moved to New York. The idea of opening a business came up at our wedding. I guess they discussed it at the reception, and by the end of our honeymoon, Cody had decided it was a great idea."

"Had you?"

"What?"

"Decided that Cody and Sean's business was a good idea."

"I wanted to support my new husband. So, yes."

"So, you didn't think it was a good idea, but went along with it to support your husband."

"I'm not that weak-willed, Jackson. Cody made a good case for the business, and I could see that it would benefit us financially. Which it did."

"But you weren't happy."

"For a while I was. New York was exciting and different."

"How about Cody? Was he happy?"

"As happy as he ever was."

"That answer begs another question," Jackson said, following the tinny GPS voice and turning onto a narrow, rutted road that led toward distant mountains.

"Cody wasn't a contented person," Morgan said. "He was always looking for something new and different. Something more than what we had."

Which sounded a whole lot like Cody was a murderer, a liar and a cheat. Jackson didn't ask what he wanted to ask. Were there other women? Other reasons why Cody may have wanted to maintain a high lifestyle? Why he may have been willing to blackmail clients for more money to support his spending habits?

There was no doubt that Morgan had thought of those things. She was a smart lady and, as she'd said, she wasn't a push-over. What she was was a woman who'd wanted the dream. The husband, the kids, the happily-ever-after. She hadn't gotten them, so she'd made a new dream for herself. An art gallery in a small town far away from the life she and her ex had. Too bad that hadn't been enough to keep her safe.

He glanced at Morgan, saw that she was staring out the side window, her dark hair hiding all but a sliver of pale cheekbone. Did she regret her marriage? Did she wish she could go back and undo what had been done? Or was she simply putting those years behind her, moving forward without regret?

More questions Jackson wouldn't ask.

What he needed to focus on was the relationship between Cody and his business partner. Murder happened for a reason.

Sometimes it was a crime of passion. Other times, it was carefully plotted out in the hope of hiding a crime or getting revenge. "Did Cody and Sean get along as business partners?"

"Usually."

"Were there specific things they didn't agree on? Maybe the way the business was being run? The direction it was headed?"

"To be honest, after the first few years, I didn't pay much attention to Cody's business. If he and Sean were disagreeing about it, I wouldn't have known."

"So, you were completely surprised when you found out that Cody had murdered his partner?"

Morgan's silence said it all, and Jackson waited it out, the dark landscape flying by for several seconds before she finally spoke. "I'd like to say I was, but I can't. Not if I'm going to be completely honest. The morning Sean was found dead in his office, I wondered."

"If Cody had killed him?"

"I don't think I could have verbalized it, but, yes."

"You were already separated."

"We were, but it wasn't just sour grapes making me want to point a finger in his direction. Cody had been unhappy for a few months before I left him. Touchy. Angry. Really difficult to be with. New Year's Eve, just a few weeks before Sean died, we were supposed to go to Sean's house for a party. I was dressed up and ready go, filled with all kinds of hope for the coming year. Cody and I had had a tough few months, but I'd resolved to try harder to make things work."

"I guess that didn't happen."

"It might have if he'd bothered coming home. He called to say he'd been held up at work. Told me he'd be home in an hour. I waited three, then packed my bags and walked out."

"I'm sorry."

"It was way past time. I'd been clinging to a dead thing for too long. Mom and Aunt Helen kept telling me that, but I refused to listen. Maybe I just wanted to prove to everyone that I hadn't made a horrible mistake when I married Cody."

"Maybe you were just a lot more loyal than your ex-husband was."

"Maybe so, but it doesn't matter. I finally did what I should have years ago and walked out. Less than a month later, Sean was dead."

"Seems like your leaving gave your ex-husband the perfect motivation for murder."

"What do you mean?"

"Do you think it's coincidence that you left him and a few weeks later he killed Sean?"

"I hadn't ever thought about it."

"So let's think about it together. Your ex acts like a jerk for a couple of months, doesn't show up to take you to a New Year's Eve party. Sounds to me like he had something on his mind. Something big."

"Really? To me it sounded like he had some*one* on his mind. And she wasn't me," Morgan responded wryly.

"That's the obvious answer, and maybe it's the right one. But let's say it isn't. Let's say something else was going on. Maybe trouble between the partners. Maybe Cody doesn't like the direction Sean is taking the business, or vise versa. He wants to get rid of his problem, but he's afraid he'll get caught."

"How would me leaving change that?"

"He wants Sean dead. He doesn't want to get caught, but he's smart enough to know he might. He's banking on getting away with murder, but if he doesn't, he needs an excuse that could keep him from being put away forever."

"A crime of passion rather than cold-blooded murder?"

"Exactly. Murder is murder, but in the eyes of the law motivation and premeditation play a big part in deciding the punishment."

"I didn't realize that."

"I bet Cody did."

"Either way, he'd be in jail."

"Yeah, but in the second scenario, he'd be in jail for a lot less time with the option of early parole for good behavior."

"Maybe I'm just too tired for this conversation, but I still don't see what difference that would make. Caught is caught, after all. And jail is jail. Besides, Cody was arrogant enough to believe he wouldn't be caught."

"So maybe he murdered Sean for another reason. Maybe Sean knew something that Cody would rather he didn't."

"Like what?"

"Whatever is on that disk."

"Which we still don't have," Morgan said, the weariness in her voice unmistakable.

"That doesn't mean we never will."

Morgan didn't respond, and Jackson let the silence between them grow. Morgan was tired. So was he. Tomorrow would be soon enough to talk more about Cody and Sean, their deaths and the disk that must somehow be connected to both of them.

For now, Jackson would simply concentrate on getting Morgan to her aunt's place and finding a way to connect to the Internet there. The sooner he began investigating Cody and his business ventures, the sooner he could find the answers he needed and the sooner he could go back to his life. The thought should have appealed to him, but it didn't.

Going back to New York meant facing his demons again; facing his failures.

It also meant leaving Morgan.

He glanced in her direction. She'd leaned her head against the window and closed her eyes. The bruises on her face, the delicate line of her jaw and neck spoke of vulnerability, but she was a strong woman. The kind who took a bad situation and made something good of it. The kind who'd faced astronomical odds and still come out a winner.

But right now, in this moment, she needed him.

And maybe *he* needed *that;* to feel he could make a difference in someone's life, effect a change the way he hadn't been able to for Lindsey.

Why else would he be worrying about going back to New York and saying goodbye to Morgan?

Because she's a beautiful woman with smarts and drive, and you'd like to spend a lot more time with her.

The thought whispered through his mind, and he pushed it aside. Not quite willing to acknowledge the truth of it.

Once he'd helped Morgan sort out the mess she was in, he'd do what he'd planned. He'd go back to Smith Mountain Lake and spend some time enjoying the peace and solitude it offered. Maybe that would clear his head. Or maybe it would just make him long for someone to share the experience with.

He scowled, turning the radio dial to an upbeat contemporary station. He hummed along to the music, but no amount of humming could silence his thoughts. They followed him as he drove deeper into the hills and toward the sanctuary he could only pray would keep Morgan safe.

TWELVE

Helen's house was tucked deep in the foothills of the Rocky Mountains. Sheltered by towering evergreens and surrounded by fifty acres of prime land, the ranch-style home had a charming appeal that hadn't faded over the years. The well-lit front porch was wide and wrapped around both sides of the house. The creamy siding seemed to gleam in the darkness. It had been years since Morgan had visited the place, but she knew it almost as well as she knew her Lakeview bungalow.

She barely waited until the car stopped before she jumped out and walked toward the porch. It felt good to stretch her legs, and it felt even better to know that she'd soon be settled into Helen's guest room. Alone.

She needed to put some distance between herself and Jackson. Traveling across country with him had forged a bond that she hadn't expected and didn't want. Hours on planes and in airports, hours of talking and learning more about one another had led her to do something she'd promised herself she'd never do again.

She'd begun to trust him, to believe in him, to pin her hopes of safety and security on him.

When they'd been sitting in his dark car, waiting while their pursuers drove by, she'd wanted nothing more than to burrow in close and to stay there. She'd let the warm weight of his arm comfort her, let herself lean on him as she hadn't leaned on anyone in years.

And she knew exactly where that would lead—heartache.

"Looks like your aunt is up and waiting," Jackson said, falling into step beside her, apparently unaware of just how desperate she was to be away from him. "I think every light in the house is on."

"She may be working. She usually forgets to turn off lights when she's in the middle of a project."

"Working at this time of night?"

"It's what she does."

"You said she was a potter."

"A fantastic one. I learned everything I know about craft from her."

"When you spent the summers here?"

"Yes. There was nothing else to do. No television. No contact with friends. Just me, Aunt Helen and the clay."

"Must have driven you crazy."

"At first," she said, smiling at the memory. Helen had offered to teach her to throw a pot six times before Morgan had finally been bored enough to accept the offer. "After a while, though, I began to enjoy the quiet and the time I spent at the pottery wheel. It filled the hours, and that was something I desperately needed." It had filled an empty spot in her heart, too. A place she hadn't even realized was empty.

She stepped onto the porch, the wide-planked floor creaking a little under her feet. The sound was the same one she'd heard when she was a teenager, and she found it comforting.

Before she could knock, the door flew open and Aunt Helen appeared. Medium-height and slender, she had deep red hair and a ready smile. "Morgan! I'm so glad you finally made it. I was beginning to worry."

"There was no need," Morgan said, doing her best to relax under her aunt's scrutiny.

"Apparently not, since you're standing right here in front of me. Are you going to introduce me to your friend?" she asked, stepping aside and gesturing for both of them to come in. Despite her smile, she looked uncomfortable, the slanted glance she shot in Jackson's direction hinting at just how unhappy she was to have a stranger staying in the house.

"This is Jackson Sharo. Jackson, this is my aunt Helen."

"A pleasure to meet you, ma'am."

"No need for the formality. Helen is fine." This time, her smile was tight and she turned away, leading Morgan and Jackson through the great room and into the kitchen. "I put some stew on the stove. It's nice and hot. Why don't you two go ahead and serve yourself while I slice some French bread? I made it this afternoon, so it's nice and fresh."

"I don't think I can eat, Aunt Helen." All Morgan wanted was to pop a pain pill and climb into bed and pray that she woke up in the morning with a fresh perspective. One that didn't include trusting Jackson to keep her safe.

"It'll do you good to get some food in you," Helen responded, handing Morgan a green glazed bowl and Jackson a blue one. Nearly matched in size and shape, they were obviously Helen's handiwork. If Morgan hadn't been so exhausted, she would have studied the pottery, looked more carefully at the design carved into the outside of the bowl before it had been fired.

Instead, she simply walked to the stove, ladled a small amount of stew into the bowl and collapsed into a chair at the kitchen table. "Thanks."

"Smells great, Helen. Did you make it yourself?" Jackson asked as he filled his own bowl and joined Morgan.

"Yes. Here. Bread and butter. Coffee." She set mugs of hot

coffee and a large oval platter on the table, dropped a butter knife down beside it and took a seat beside Morgan. "You look terrible, kid."

"Gee. Thanks."

"I'd like to get my hands on that no-good ex-husband of yours."

"That will be difficult, Aunt Helen. He's dead."

"Cody? Dead? Since when?"

"A few days ago. He was murdered in prison."

"Guess felons aren't nearly as forgiving as you always were."

"I was doing what I thought was right." Morgan shoveled in a spoonful of stew, refusing to enter into the argument Helen obviously wanted to start. It was one they'd fought on too many occasions during the first years of Morgan's marriage, and it had eventually put a wedge between them that no amount of time seemed to be able to remove.

"You were. He wasn't. And I can't feel sorry that he's dead."

"Helen!"

"It's the truth. He deserved what he got."

"I'm not sure anyone deserves to be murdered. Even someone like Cody," Jackson interrupted, grabbing a piece of bread and buttering it. Acting as if he were completely unaware of the tension that filled the room.

He wasn't. Morgan was sure of that. Just as she was sure he'd been right to think they'd been followed from the airport. He had instinct and guts, and those were qualities Morgan couldn't help but admire, but that didn't mean she should admire the man or allow herself to be attracted to him. She'd do well to keep that in mind.

"A murderer doesn't deserve his punishment?" Helen asked, her deep green eyes flashing with anger, and Morgan smiled. Helen was known for a lot of things. Her artistic talent, her solitary ways, her generosity of spirit.

Her temper.

She'd let Helen and Jackson duke it out for a while. At least that would take the attention off her.

"Cody was serving his time," Jackson said. "Much as I agree the guy was scum, I don't think that means he deserved to be murdered."

"So, I guess you don't believe in an eye for an eye," Helen said, sipping coffee from a thick red mug, her face tight with irritation.

"I believe in letting the system do its work. That happened. If he'd lived, Cody would have spent the rest of his life behind bars. Some people would say that's a worse fate than death."

"I can't say I agree. Thirty years in jail sounds a whole lot better to me than a long, slow burn in he—"

"Helen!" Morgan cut her aunt off before she could go any further.

"Sorry, kid. I'm not trying to pick a fight over this."

"Yes, you are," Morgan said, standing and bringing her bowl to the sink.

"Okay. I am. I like a good debate."

"And I like a little peace and quiet when my head feels like it's going to explode from pain," Morgan muttered.

"How about I get you some Tylenol?"

"I've got some prescription medicine in my bag. I'll just get it from the car." She left the kitchen, started to open the front door.

"I'll get it." Jackson's hand landed on her shoulder, holding her in place.

"I'm perfectly capable of—"

"That's got nothing to do with it, Morgan. You going outside alone isn't a good idea."

Morgan thought of the car slowly passing them, the fear thrumming through her as she'd imagined it stopping, imagined men pouring out of it. Imagined bullets flying, Jackson falling. Herself being herded away, captured again. This time with no hope for escape.

Maybe letting Jackson get the bag wasn't such a bad idea, after all. "All right. Thanks."

He smiled, his auburn hair slightly mussed. She wanted to smooth it down, let her hands trail from his head to his neck and then his shoulders. She wanted to feel the firm muscles beneath his button-down shirt. Wanted to twine her arms around his waist, let herself enjoy the strength and comfort she knew he would offer if she asked.

But she wouldn't.

Couldn't.

She turned on her heels, ran from Jackson, racing into the kitchen, her face flaming hot with emotions she did *not* want to feel.

She had no room for a man in her life. No room in her heart.

"Everything okay?" Helen asked as Morgan rushed back into the kitchen.

"Fine."

"So, where'd you pick up the new guy?"

"I didn't pick him up."

"You know what I mean."

"We met last night. He saved my life."

"And then flew across the country with you because…?"

"My friends were worried about me, and Jackson assured them he'd keep me safe."

"Seriously? He saved your life and now he's playing body-guard?" Helen's gaze darted to the great room, as if she expected Jackson to be standing there listening.

"I tried to get rid of him, but he refused to go."

"Romantic."

"Annoying."

"I'd snort if it weren't too unladylike."

"Since when did you care about being ladylike? Besides, what is there to snort about?"

"The fact that you don't think the story you just told me is romantic. Man saves woman's life. Man promises to keep her safe. It's classic. And almost worth having the guy stay at my house."

"Almost?"

"You know I don't do strangers. If it weren't for the fact that I haven't seen you in years, I'd have told you to take your guy friend over to your parents' and leave him there."

"You haven't changed, Aunt Helen."

"Neither have you. I'm glad. I was worried that jerk of a husband of yours might have done some damage."

"He did," Morgan said, reaching for her coffee mug and taking a sip, hoping the hot liquid would wash away the lump in her throat.

"Just enough to make you stronger," Helen covered Morgan's hand with hers, smiled gently.

"Knock, knock, I'm back," Jackson called, and Morgan stood, turning to face him as he entered the room. Bracing herself for the quick shiver of awareness that shot through her as she met his eyes.

Romantic?

Not hardly. *Terrifying* was more the word Morgan would use.

"Want me to bring it to your room?" Jackson asked as he set the carry-on down by her feet.

"No, thanks." She unzipped the front compartment, pulled out the bottle of pills she'd picked up before Lacey and Jude's wedding and popped the lid.

Helen handed her a glass of water, and Morgan swallowed one of the tablets, hoping that it would begin working soon. The pain in her cheek and jaw had been getting progressively worse during the day, and her entire body seemed to ache. Her ribs. Her throat. Her arms and legs.

"I've got your room all ready for you, Morgan. Same one you stayed in when you were a kid. Why don't you go climb into bed? You'll feel better in the morning," Helen said, taking Morgan's arm.

"I think I will. We can do some more catching up in the morning."

"Where's your room? I'll walk you there." Jackson lifted the carry-on again.

"Just off the family room, but I can manage the carry-on myself."

"That's not the reason I want to walk you to your room. It'll be a lot easier to keep you safe if I know exactly where you are."

"She'll be safe enough, Jackson. The doors all have bolts and the windows are double paned."

"Even the best locks can't keep everyone out," Jackson responded.

"That's why I've got Mutton and Ox."

"Mutton and Ox?"

"My mastiffs. They're out in the barn for now, but I'll bring them in the house after I get the two of you settled. They wouldn't hurt a fly, but their barks and their looks are enough to put most people off."

"Since when do you like dogs?" Morgan asked, remembering the summers when she'd begged for a puppy.

"Since right around the time I decided that I could like them and bring a couple home or spend the rest of my life talking to myself. I love my solitude, but a little company now and again isn't such a bad thing." Helen smiled and walked to the hall that led to the east wing of the house.

Morgan followed, Jackson just a few steps behind.

She could feel his presence. Feel the warmth of his gaze as she made her way to the east wing of the rancher and into a wide hall with several doors opening from it. Three led to spacious bedrooms. One led to the pottery shed where Morgan had learned to throw clay. If she were alone, she'd be tempted to go there, grab a block of clay and knead it into compliance. Clay, after all, was something she could control most of the time. When she couldn't, she could simply reshape it, try again to make it into what she wanted it to be.

But she wasn't alone, and she didn't feel like explaining her desire to create to Jackson. Nor was she in the mood to chat with Helen while she shaped a pot or vase or whatever vessel the clay formed.

"I haven't changed much of anything around here. A few more pieces of pottery. That's about it, but it's clean, and I put fresh sheets on the bed while I was waiting for you." Helen shrugged as she pushed open the door to the room.

Morgan stepped across the threshold, appreciating the timeless elegance of the room as she hadn't when she was a teenager. Sage-green walls. Dark wood floors. French doors covered by breezy white drapes. White bed linens and shelves of pottery in every color and size and shape.

"Wow!" Jackson let out a low whistle and stepped into the room after Morgan, setting down the carry-on. "You've got quite a collection of pottery, Helen."

"It's not just a collection. They're her work," Morgan said, knowing that her aunt wouldn't bother correcting Jackson's assumption.

"They're beautiful. Morgan told me you were a potter, but I had no idea of the scope of your work."

"Thank you, but they're not all mine. Some are Morgan's."

"Really? Which are which?" he asked, lifting a butter yellow vase with a surface as smooth and slick as oil.

"That's Aunt Helen's. Mine are a whole lot less refined."

"You'd only just begun to work with clay, so they weren't perfect, but they were lovely. This is one of hers. The first piece she ever made," Helen said, reaching for a large blue bowl. Its fluted edges were uneven, the glaze spotty at best.

"I can't believe you kept that," Morgan said, taking the piece from her aunt. The surface was slightly rough and uneven, but the weight felt comfortable in her hands.

"Of course I kept it. I figured eventually you'd be famous, and I could make a hefty sum off the piece. So don't drop it. I'd hate to see my retirement fund swept up and thrown in the garbage." Helen smiled, taking the bowl and setting it back on the shelf.

"Retirement fund? You'll be lucky to get a dollar for it."

"You never did give yourself enough credit. Come on, Jackson, let's let my niece get some rest. Good night, Morgan."

"Good night," Morgan responded, as her aunt moved out into the hall.

"Are you going to be okay?" Jackson asked, moving close, his hands gentle on her shoulders as he looked down into her eyes. She wanted to shake her head, do what she'd longed to earlier and throw herself into his arms. She took a step back instead.

"Of course."

"Then why do you look so scared?"

"Because I am, but I can't let it control me. If I do, I'll climb into bed, cover my head with a blanket and never come out."

"There's nothing to be afraid of, Morgan. Not tonight, anyway. If someone did follow us from the airport, we lost him, and it won't be easy for him to find us here. Even if he does, your aunt's dogs will give us an early warning before he even tries to break in. Of course, if you're still worried, I can park outside your door for the night."

"I'm not *that* worried."

He chuckled, letting his hands fall away. "I kind of figured you'd say that. So, I'll be wherever your aunt puts me."

He walked out into the hallway, and Morgan had to force herself not to grab his arm to keep him from going.

She was an adult, after all. Perfectly capable of being alone at night regardless of what she'd been through, and perfectly capable of ignoring the way she felt whenever Jackson was around.

She opened her carry-on, pulled out pajamas, toothpaste and toothbrush and walked into the adjoining bathroom. After a long day's travel, a shower was probably a good idea, but she didn't have the energy for it. She changed quickly, brushing her teeth, washing her face and calling that good enough.

The house had fallen silent. No creaking floors or whispered voices. Just the easy quiet that came from a full house gone to sleep. That was one thing she'd missed about her parents' home. Knowing that someone else was always just a word away.

Outside, the wind had picked up. It howled beneath the eves and moaned through the trees. To Morgan it was the music of the mountains, and it filled her with a sense of peace she hadn't had in a long time. At least here, far from the sounds of city life, far from the demands of a business that would thrive or die by her hands, Morgan could hear the rhythm of her breathing and of her thoughts. She could picture the sweet face of little Katia, the wise, strong face of Nikolai, and somehow they intertwined with the faces of her family in Washington. Benjamin, Lauren, Josh and Joseph, Mom and Dad and Helen. They were faces of people she loved and of people she'd missed.

So why had it taken her so long to return to them?

She sighed. The pain was beginning to ease, and she knew she should sleep, but sleep had never come easily to Morgan. She paced the room for a few minutes, then went to the French doors, pulling back the curtains and staring into the darkness. Tall evergreens stretched toward the deep black sky, their spindly branches and narrow trunks bending beneath the howling wind. Morgan was tempted to open the French doors, walk outside and lose herself in the darkness for a while. Try to forget the men who were after her, the disk Cody had hidden and the fear that had chased her from Lakeview.

A soft tapping came from beyond the bedroom door, and Morgan stiffened, straining to hear more. A quiet bark, a mumbled word. A door opening and closing. Then silence again.

Helen and her dogs retiring for the night.

If someone was outside waiting for an opportunity to strike, the dogs wouldn't be so eager to quiet down. Like Jackson had said, if someone had tried to follow them from the airport, the attempt hadn't been successful. The road behind them had been empty for the last twenty miles of their journey.

So, why not go outside until the pain medication finished doing its work, sit on the swing that hung from the ceiling beams of the back porch? She'd be close enough to the house to run inside if she sensed danger.

She grabbed a jacket from her carry-on, shoved her feet into slippers and opened the French doors. There was a light switch inside her room, but she didn't bother to turn on the outside lights. Cold, fresh air slapped her cheeks and stung her eyes as she felt her way to the edge of the porch and the swing that hung there. Though she couldn't see it, she could picture the painted wood and cushioned bench, the thick chains that attached it to the ceiling. They groaned a protest as Morgan settled onto the seat, and she smiled, remembering all the nights she'd spent sitting alone on the porch, enjoying the cool summer breeze, dreaming of the day she'd be reunited with Katia and Nikolai.

Those dreams hadn't come true, but she was back on the swing, inhaling the first hints of winter in the gusting wind.

She'd almost died without knowing what had happened to the two people she'd loved most when she was a kid. The two people who'd lived what she'd lived, experienced what she had. She was connected to them in a way she wasn't connected to anyone else.

Maybe it was time to dream again.

She leaned her head against the back of the swing, and

closed her eyes. She'd renew her search to find Katia and Nikolai, but first she had to find the disk that Cody had hidden. Considering how little she actually knew about her husband and his business dealings, that would be like looking for a needle in a haystack.

"Any help you want to give me would be great, Lord," she muttered, wondering just how effective her prayer would be. It seemed like she spent a lot of time asking God for help, but not nearly as much trying to ascertain His will for her life. It wasn't the way her parents had raised her. Their faith was as strong and unwavering as the mountains that surrounded their house. Morgan's was much more fickle. She believed in God, believed the message of salvation she'd professed when she was twelve, but she didn't always believe that God was eager and willing to step in and save the day.

She sighed, knowing she should go back in the house and get some sleep. The pain medication was doing its work, the throbbing agony of her injuries now a muted ache, but the swing was comfortable, the memories it invoked more pleasant than painful, and she stayed where she was as the wind continued to howl and the first drops of rain began to fall.

THIRTEEN

Jackson scanned one of several dozen online articles about Cody Bradshaw's trial and frowned. There'd been plenty written about Morgan. Speculation about her affair with Sean and about what she might gain from having her husband go to jail. The media had painted her in an unforgiving light, citing sources who claimed to have the inside scoop and who were quick to point out that Morgan had filed for divorce before Cody was arrested. She was, they'd said, a black widow. A woman who made her living preying on the men in her life.

No wonder Morgan had been anxious to leave New York.

He pulled up another article, skimming it for any details that hadn't been in the last few he'd read. There was nothing.

He scowled, logging off the computer and pacing the den. It was late and calling the East Coast would have to wait several hours. In the meantime, Jackson should sleep. He should, but his mind was humming with questions that begged answers.

Who?

Why?

Those were the two most pressing ones. Until he could answer them, Morgan wouldn't be safe.

Until *he* could answer them?

There were plenty of people working the case. Since when had it become his responsibility to solve it?

That was another question that begged answers, but it wasn't one that Jackson was all that anxious to explore.

He frowned, raking a hand over his hair and eyeing the pullout sofa Helen had made up for him. A few hours of sleep would clear his head and put him in a better frame of mind to tackle the case. He dropped down onto the mattress and lay staring up at the ceiling, the questions he'd been asking for the past two days circling around in his mind, refusing to let him sink into sleep.

Cody Bradshaw had information that was dangerous to someone. Jackson knew it. All he had to do was get his hands on the disk and he'd know exactly what the information was and exactly why someone was willing to commit murder to retrieve it.

Outside, the wind had abated, but the rain that had begun an hour ago continued, the soft patter as it hit the roof mixing with the creaks and groans of the house settling. A soft hum was audible just below the other sounds. Not a person. Maybe a machine?

Curious, Jackson stood, stretching the kinks from his neck and back as he followed the sound through the den and into the great room with its vaulted ceilings and stone fireplace. The kitchen was visible from here, the stainless steel appliances and sleek granite counter a stark contrast to the old-fashioned feel of the rest of the house. Like her niece, Helen wasn't someone who could be easily pegged.

The hum grew louder as Jackson stepped into the wide hall that led to Morgan's room. It seemed to be coming from the closest room, and he walked to it, bending his head close and listening. The hum was definitely mechanical. Not a washing machine or dryer. Something else. Maybe Jackson wasn't the only one who couldn't sleep. He was tempted to knock and see who came to the door, but the thought of pulling Helen from whatever she was doing wasn't nearly as appealing as the thought of pulling Morgan away from something.

A quiet huff sounded from the other side of the door, and Jackson backed away as a dog barked, the deep rumble of sound telling him exactly who was in the room. Helen murmured something to the animal and it quieted, but she didn't come to the door to see who was roaming the hall.

Maybe she knew.

Or maybe she assumed it was Morgan.

Morgan, who should be sleeping soundly in the room just down the hall.

Was she?

If so, she was the only one who wasn't awake and restless, too filled with thoughts and worries to sleep.

Jackson knew that walking down the hall and knocking on Morgan's door was the last thing that he should do. What he should do, what he needed to do was turn around, go back to the den and do his best to fall asleep.

It was what he should do, but for reasons he wouldn't name, he didn't.

Instead, he walked to Morgan's door, pressed his ear close to it and listened. He heard nothing but the hum of whatever machine Helen was working on and the tap of rain on the roof. Nothing to make him think Morgan was awake. He knocked anyway, the sound soft enough that it would only carry to someone inside the room. Someone awake enough to hear it.

When Morgan didn't respond, Jackson turned to leave. Then hesitated. Making assumptions wasn't something he believed in doing. Morgan could be sleeping, or she could be wide awake like everyone else in the house. Wide awake and at loose ends. In her position, he'd be tempted to walk out the double French doors, let the crisp mountain air clear his head. The thought of Morgan wandering around outside in the storm was enough to have him knocking again.

He waited, then twisted the doorknob and opened the door just enough to get a clear view of the room. Dark and quiet, it looked exactly as it had when Jackson had entered it an hour ago. Crisp white bedding smooth and rumple free.

He frowned, opening the door wider and striding into the room. Morgan had left the carry-on open on the floor, left the door to the adjoining bathroom open to reveal another empty space.

She *had* gone outside.

Jackson's pulse jumped, his stomach twisting as he imagined her walking around in the mountain wilderness. It wasn't nature that worried him. Bears, coyotes, wolves and mountain lions weren't nearly the threat that man could be.

He crossed the room, yanking open the French doors so hard they slammed against the wall. Rain splashed onto the ground and the roof as he stepped out onto a wide porch, the sound filling the sheltered area. Jackson waited impatiently as his eyes adjusted to the darkness, his ears picking up other sounds. The rustle of leaves, the creak of tree branches, a soft shuffling sound that didn't fit with the others.

He tensed, turning as a black shadow lunged from the darkness to his right, darted out into the rain. Jackson followed, splashing through mud and puddles, grabbing the back of a jacket, ready to throw himself against the intruder, knock him off his feet.

Except that the intruder looked to be about five-four, maybe a hundred and five pounds.

"Morgan?" He yanked on the jacket, tugging her back and hearing fabric tear as she fought to free herself. "Morgan! It's me. Jackson."

It took a second for his words to sink in. When they finally did, she stopped struggling and turned on him, her pale face barely visible in the darkness, the fist she was swinging just missing his jaw.

He grabbed her hand, gently pulling it down before she could take another shot at him. "Hey, I'm not one of the bad guys."

"No, you're just the guy who scared a decade off my life. What were you thinking coming out here?" Her voice shook, and Jackson pulled her into his arms, pressing her head against his chest, trying to still her trembling and offer the comfort she seemed to need.

"I could ask you the same thing, but I think I know the answer."

She stiffened, pulled back. "I couldn't sleep. Too much has happened, and I'm still wound up from it all. It's as simple as that."

"I wasn't suggesting anything else." But it was interesting that she'd thought he had been. Maybe the danger she was in wasn't the only thing that had been keeping Morgan awake. Maybe, like Jackson, she was wondering what was happening between them.

And there *was* something happening, whether they wanted to admit it or not.

"Come on," he said, knowing that she wouldn't want to hear his thoughts. "Let's get back on the porch before we're both soaked."

"I think it's too late for that."

"So maybe we can grab a couple of towels from your bathroom and dry off." He released his hold and stepped back, offering Morgan a hand.

She hesitated, then accepted, her palm icy as he hurried her up the stairs and into her room.

"Wait here. I'll get the towels," she said, rushing into the bathroom and shutting the door.

Maybe he should walk out of her room, go back to the den and dry off there.

That was the safe thing to do. Maybe even the right thing,

but Jackson couldn't leave. Not until he knew Morgan was really as fine as she always claimed to be.

The bathroom door swung open, and she reappeared, a towel wrapped around her head, a thick terry cloth robe covering what looked like heavy flannel pajamas. She was still dripping, rain water trickling from the hem of the pajamas and pooling at her feet. Despite the bruises, she was breathtaking, her skin smooth and tan, her eyes such a striking blue Jackson thought he could stare into them all night and never get tired of looking.

He took a step toward her, stopping himself just short of doing what he wanted—pulling her into his arms again.

Maybe sticking around hadn't been such a good idea.

"Here you go." She tossed him a handful of towels, and he caught them, using one to wipe water from his face and wishing it would clear his muddled brain, too.

"Thanks."

"It's the least I can do, since it's my fault you ran out into the storm. You never did tell me why you were awake," she said absently as she pulled the towel from her head and rubbed her hair dry with it.

And Jackson decided a full retreat was his best option.

"I think I'll grab a cup of coffee to warm up." He spun around and walked out the door, hoping Morgan wouldn't follow.

Hoping she would.

"Were you looking for information about Cody? I know you said you were going to, but I figured you'd get some sleep first," she said as she walked into the kitchen behind him.

"I decided there was no time like the present to start digging, so I did some online research."

"Find anything?" she asked a little too nonchalantly. She knew what was in the newspaper reports, knew what she'd been accused of and what public opinion about her had been during her husband's trial. No doubt, she was waiting for him to bring it up, but Jackson didn't see any sense in doing so.

"Nothing that will help. As soon as it's a decent hour, I'm going to call Cody's parents. See if they'll be willing to answer a few questions."

"Good luck. Like I said before, they only do what benefits them," she responded, grabbing coffee from a cupboard and starting a pot.

"They were brutal to you during Cody's trial."

"They weren't easy to get along with at the best of times. After their son went to trial, they needed a scapegoat. I was it."

"That had to be rough."

"Not really. I expected it. As long as the jury found Cody guilty, I didn't care what anyone thought of me."

She poured coffee, handed him a cup. "How about we take it back out on the porch? I don't want to disturb Aunt Helen."

He knew he should say no. Knew he should suggest that Morgan go back to her room and he go back to his.

He didn't.

And that told him more than he wanted to know about what direction his relationship with Morgan was going and just how far over the line of professionalism he'd crossed.

"Sure. Why not?"

They walked silently through the hall, back through Morgan's bedroom and out onto the porch.

"There's a swing over here. It might be a little wet. The wind has been blowing the rain onto the porch," Morgan said, her voice holding a hint of the uncertainty Jackson was feeling.

Sitting on the porch swing together was different than sitting on a plane or in a car, or even standing in Morgan's room chatting. It was an acknowledgement of what they both felt, an agreement that what they were forging was more than just business, more than just a joint effort to find the men who were after Morgan.

Jackson knew it, but he went anyway, taking Morgan's hand and leading her to the swing, brushing the moisture off with the towel he'd hung around his neck. Then folding the towel and gesturing for her to sit on it.

"That's very gentlemanly of you," she said, laughing nervously as she took a seat.

"My mother will be happy to hear that you said that."

"She doesn't think you're a gentleman?"

"She's hopeful, but not always convinced."

"Are you close?"

"Yes, but it's been harder since my sister died. When we're together, me and my parents, there's always a feeling that someone is missing. That we aren't complete." He settled onto the bench beside her, felt her stiffen, then relax.

"I know how difficult that is. I've spent most of my life feeling the same way."

"The difference is, there is every chance that your brother and sister are out there somewhere, waiting for you to find them."

"I've spent a lot of time trying to do just that, but I keep coming up empty."

"I meant what I said about helping you, Morgan. All I'll need are their names and birth dates. The city and country of birth."

"I'll give you what I have. It's not much."

"Not much is more than what I've gone on before. I can't promise results, but I'll try my best."

"You're already doing too much." But she didn't tell him not to try, and her hand slipped into his, her fingers squeezing gently before she released her hold. He wanted to capture it again, bring it to his lips and press a kiss to her knuckles. But that would be too much too soon!

"We should go back inside now. You did promise your sister that you'd be at church, and that's not too many hours from now."

"I know." She didn't get up, though. Just sat completely still, her head resting against the back of the swing. In profile, her face was delicate, the angle of her jaw sharply defined. She looked lost in thought, caught up in her memories, but completely relaxed and more at ease than he'd ever seen her before.

"Is this a place you spent a lot of time when you were a kid?"

"Nearly every night during the summer for four years. Helen doesn't believe in television. She says it distracts from creativity."

"So you sat out here instead of sitting in front of the television?"

"Not quite."

"That sounds interesting."

"It isn't. While Helen worked, I'd wander around in the woods behind the house. Eventually, I'd end up back here, and I'd sit on the swing and listen."

"To?"

"My own thoughts. That was something I didn't get much time to do during the school year. Mom and Dad are great, and my siblings were fun, but the ranch was always loud and busy. When I was here, I could actually hear myself think."

"What—"

Jackson didn't get a chance to finish the question. Somewhere inside the house, a dog barked. Another joined it, the frantic cadence of their tone clearly a warning.

Jackson stood quickly, grabbed Morgan's hand and pulled her to her feet. "Come on."

She held on, running with him as he sprinted the few feet to the French doors.

"Go inside. Lock the doors and call the police."

"But—"

"Don't go near the windows or doors. Don't come outside."

"You're not staying out there," Morgan protested as Jackson gave her a gentle nudge into the room.

But he was, and he handed her his coffee cup and shut the door, silencing her protest.

The dogs continued to bark, the sound edging along Jackson's nerves as he surveyed the dark yard, cocked his head to the side and listened.

A car engine rumbled in the distance, the sound growing louder. Was that what had alarmed the dogs?

If so, it was a better scenario than the one Jackson had been imagining. Armed gunmen surrounding the house, coming in with barrels blazing. Killing Jackson and Helen, torturing Morgan until she gave them what they wanted or died.

No way did Jackson plan to die, and no way did he plan to let either of the women in the house die, so he'd have to find out who was in the approaching vehicle. If that person planned to cause trouble, Jackson would stop him.

He jumped off the porch and rounded the side of the house, rain soaking his head and shirt as he made his way to the front yard and crouched in the shadows beneath a huge pine. His hand itched for the gun he'd left back in Lakeview, and he tensed as headlights appeared in the distance. Heading toward the house. In just a few minutes the car would be on him. Jackson slipped behind the tree's wide trunk, pressing close. Watching. Waiting.

Praying.

That he could keep Morgan safe. That he could help her find the answers she so desperately needed. That God would give him the time he needed to do it.

FOURTEEN

Morgan ran through her room and out into the hall, slamming into someone, coffee cups dropping from her hands, a scream tearing from her throat.

"Morgan!" Helen nearly shrieked. "Are you okay?"

"Yes, but there's someone outside."

"I know. The dogs are going crazy. We need to get Jackson, let him know what's going on." The hall light went on, and Morgan blinked.

"He already knows. We were out on the back porch together when the dogs started barking." She spoke without thinking, and she regretted it immediately.

"I see."

"There's nothing to see, Aunt Helen. I was awake. So was he."

"I believe you. Even if I didn't, it's none of my business. Where is Jackson now? It's probably for the best if we all stick together until the police get here."

"You called them?"

"Of course. The dogs start barking like crazy, and I take that seriously. Especially considering what you went through last night. So, where's our hero?"

"Still outside. He wants us to wait in here until the police arrive."

"I like his plan."

"I don't," Morgan said, walking into the great room and wanting desperately to keep walking. Through the room, into the foyer and out the front door. Jackson shouldn't be outside facing danger himself. Not when it was Morgan's trouble he was walking into.

"Do you have a better one?"

"Yes, we find a couple of weapons, and we go outside to give Jackson a hand."

"Sorry. I'm fresh out of weapons."

"What about the gun you used to keep in the box under your bed?"

"How did you know about that?"

"What do you think I was doing while you were working in the studio day after day and night after night when I was a kid?"

"I hoped you were reading a book or looking at a magazine, or maybe working on your own art projects."

"I was snooping. So, do you still have the gun?"

"Yes."

"Good. I'll run and get it."

"Knock yourself out, but it won't do any good. The gun isn't loaded and I've never had bullets for it."

"What? Then why keep it?"

"To scare away intruders."

"So maybe we can use it for the same," Morgan muttered, hurrying into her aunt's room.

She slid down onto her stomach, grabbing the box with shaking hands and pulling the pistol from it. She'd never liked guns, but having one could be the difference between life and death. Tomorrow, she'd find out what kind of bullets the weapon needed and she'd buy some.

If she lived until tomorrow.

If Jackson and Helen did.

The thought of them both lying dead in pools of blood filled Morgan with sick dread, and she hurried back out of the room, the dogs still barking frantically, the sound digging deep into her brain and renewing the throbbing pulse of pain there.

She yanked open the front door, stumbling when Helen pulled her backward.

"You can't go out there," Helen said, trying to hold her in place.

"Of course I can," Morgan responded, tugging from her grasp, racing out into the rain. Bright headlights illuminated the dirt road a few hundred yards away as a car slowly eased toward the house.

Could the driver see her?

Terrified, Morgan dropped to her belly, the wet ground soaking her clothes through and leaving her shivering with cold.

She needed to move. Get to a place where she couldn't be seen, but she was frozen in place, the worry and adrenaline that had sent her running from the house, gone. In its place there was nothing but fear.

"What are you doing out here?" Jackson hissed from somewhere in the darkness, his voice so unexpected Morgan jumped.

"Looking for you." She shifted, trying to see him, oddly comforted by his voice. Maybe facing death was easier to do with a partner.

The grim thought barely had time to register as the car stopped.

Morgan braced herself, expecting the doors to fly open, men to spill out into the night. Her heart beat hard with fear, her hand fisted around the gun as she waited for the nightmare to continue.

To her right, a branch broke and grass rustled. Something dark and low moved toward her, the slow, lithe movements almost snakelike. The form human. Large. Jackson? Someone else?

Fear twisted in Morgan's stomach, and she lifted the gun, her hand shaking so hard she was sure she'd drop it.

"Put that down before it goes off." Jackson's voice cut through the darkness again, and Morgan nearly sagged with relief.

"It's not loaded."

"Then I guess it won't do us much good," Jackson said, sliding up beside her and taking the gun from her hand.

"What are they doing? Why is the car just sitting there?"

"Maybe the driver is scoping the place out. Which works out well, because I'm going to scope him out. Stay here. And this time, really stay." Jackson moved away, disappearing back into the darkness and leaving Morgan alone again.

No gun in her hand.

No weapon of any kind.

She scanned the area, searching for Jackson, but he'd moved quickly and silently and was as invisible as air. Too bad she wasn't as good at disappearing. She could slip into the woods that surrounded the house, find a hiding place and stay there until everything blew over.

The car engine revved and Morgan tensed, expecting the vehicle to jump forward, maybe slam into Helen's house. Instead, it did a quick U-turn and raced away.

Morgan jumped to her feet, her heart pounding as the car rounded a curve and disappeared from view. Gone as quickly as it had come.

Had Jackson gotten a look at the driver?

She glanced around, saw him walking toward her, a black shadow against the darkness. "Did you see him?"

"Them. Two men. I didn't see much else before they took off."

"Did they see you?"

"No. I think they got what they wanted and decided to leave."

"If what they wanted was to scare the wits out of me, then they definitely got it."

"I think they were more interested in getting the lay of the land."

"So they can figure out the best way to launch an attack?"

"Maybe. What they weren't counting on is someone being outside and close enough to get a look at the license plate number."

"Did you?"

"Yes. Come on," he said, taking her arm. "The faster I can get the police searching for that car, the more likely it will be found."

The door flew open before they reached it, and Helen ran out, a cast-iron skillet in her hand. "The police are on the way. They should be here any minute."

"Too bad our friends decided to leave then," Jackson responded, hurrying Morgan into the house as he pulled a cell phone from his pocket.

"Were you planning to use the skillet to protect us?" Morgan asked her aunt, dropping onto the couch, her heart still pounding frantically.

"It was that or a knife. This I could throw with some accuracy." Helen set the skillet onto the coffee table, frowning in Jackson's direction. "He's calling the police again?"

"He saw the license plate number of the car and thinks it's better to call it in now than wait until the police arrive."

"Well, that's something at least. I guess if my little sanctuary has got to be invaded, that'll make it worthwhile."

"I'm sorry we barged in on you tonight, Aunt Helen. I know you prefer your solitude. And I'm especially sorry that I've brought my troubles with me."

"Your troubles are my troubles. That's the way it is with family."

"Not when it means putting someone I love in danger. I should have stayed in Lakeview." Or gone back to New York. Or taken the first flight out of the country.

"Of course you shouldn't have. Your family is here. And whether you want to admit it or not, you need us now."

Needed them?

She loved her family. She appreciated them. But she'd never wanted to need them, had never wanted to be that vulnerable.

Outside, sirens screamed, announcing the arrival of the

police, and Helen hurried to the front door and pulled it open, waiting in the threshold for the officers to get out of their cars.

Morgan stayed put, her energy gone, her mind numb.

She'd thought she would be safe in her aunt's mountain home, but the danger she'd fled had followed her. She frowned, rubbing at the tension in the back of her neck.

"You okay?" Jackson dropped onto the couch beside her, a scowl hardening his features. The charming man of a few hours ago was gone. In his place was someone much more dangerous, but just as compelling.

Morgan resisted the urge to scoot to the other end of the couch and put a few extra inches of space between them.

"I'm fine," she managed to say, meeting his eyes and offering a smile she didn't feel. She wasn't all right. She hadn't been all right in a long time, but that wasn't something she planned to share with anyone.

"The police are putting out an APB on our guys' car."

"I hope they find it soon. I'm not made for intrigue and danger."

"I doubt many people are, but you're tough, Morgan. You'll handle whatever comes your way, and you'll come out on top."

Jackson was right. She *was* tough. She'd had to be. But sometimes being tough got tiring. Sometimes she wanted nothing more than to have someone to lean on. Someone who could fight her battles for her.

She'd thought Cody would be that person. She'd been wrong. Risking her heart and her emotions wasn't something she planned to ever do again.

But if she did, Jackson was the kind of person she imagined she'd want to do it with.

And that was a direction she should not be letting her mind go.

She stood. "I think I'll go see why it's taking the police so long to come in."

Jackson grabbed her hand, stopping her before she could

walk away. "They're collecting evidence outside before they come in. There's nothing we can do out there but get in the way."

"Then I'll—"

"You don't have to run away, Morgan. I'm not going to bite."

"I wasn't running."

"You were leaving. I guess I wonder why."

"I already told you."

"You gave me an excuse, but I think there's another reason."

"And I guess you're going to tell me what it is?"

"Just what I told you when we were on the plane. I think I make you uncomfortable."

"Why would you think that?"

"Because you make *me* uncomfortable, and I was thinking the feeling might be mutual."

His honesty surprised Morgan, disarmed her, and she frowned, pulling her hand from his. "We're both tired, Jackson. It's been a long twenty-four hours, we're under an incredible amount of stress."

"So we're making something out of nothing and we really aren't attracted to each other?"

"I didn't say anything about being attracted."

"I did."

"Well, you can unsay it, because I'm not. We're not." Morgan turned on her heels and hurried to Helen's side, refusing to acknowledge the way her pulse had leaped when Jackson had looked into her eyes, the way her heart had jumped when he'd said he was attracted to her.

There were more important things to think about. Things that could be the difference between living and dying. She needed to find the disk Cody had hidden, needed to turn it over to the police and needed to go back to her quiet pottery gallery in Lakeview, her quiet life and her search for Katia and Nikolai.

As she stood next to Helen, watching several flashlights bob and sway along the driveway, Morgan prayed that God would give her the opportunity to do all three.

FIFTEEN

It didn't take long for the police to collect evidence outside the house. Probably because there wasn't much to collect. The interviews took a little longer, and Jackson bit back impatience as the three officers asked the same questions over and over again. It was par for the course, but that didn't make him any happier.

"So, you think you were followed from Virginia because someone wants the disk your husband said you have?" the oldest of the three asked Morgan, his grizzled face and salt-and-pepper hair speaking of years of experience.

"Yes," Morgan responded, sounding a lot less irritated than Jackson felt.

Helen, on the other hand, looked like she was about to explode. Five-nine, maybe a hundred and twenty pounds, she was thin to the point of gauntness, her pale face surrounded by fiery hair, her green eyes blazing with the same heat. She was young. Much younger than Jackson had expected her to be. In his mind, she'd been fiftyish with gray hair and a plain, round face, bustling around in long, flowing flower-print dresses and scuffed brown sandals.

As if she sensed his gaze, she threw a sharp look in his direction. He didn't bother looking away. Morgan was his top priority. Protecting her meant knowing about her life and the people in it. Including her taciturn aunt.

"We've already contacted the Lakeview Sheriff's Department to let them know what's gone on here tonight, and we want to assure you that we're cooperating fully with their investigation," the officer said, giving a we're-finished-here spiel that pulled Jackson's attention back to the interview and away from Helen.

"I appreciate that, officer," Morgan responded, standing up and moving toward the front door.

"We'll run patrol cars down this road a few times before morning. Keep the doors and windows locked, and don't hesitate to call if you're worried. The dogs bark, you hear strange noises. Call. It's always better to be safe than sorry." He walked outside and let the other two officers step off the porch before turning his attention to Jackson. "Do you have a weapon, Mr. Sharo?"

"Not unless you count an unloaded handgun that we've got no ammunition for." He gestured to the weapon, lying on the coffee table.

"I wouldn't recommend this for everyone, but you were a police officer and a military man. You know your way around a gun. You might want to get some ammunition." He stepped off the porch, and Jackson followed, hearing the warning the officer hadn't voiced. The house wasn't easy to get to. It might take time for a responding officer to arrive. Too much time.

Rain still fell, a chilly wind howling through the towering pines and cutting through Jackson's wet shirt. He'd have to find a place to buy some clothes, but first he needed to make some phone calls. It was six in the morning on the East Coast. Early, but Jackson wouldn't let that bother him.

He waited until the officers drove away, then pulled out his cell phone, checking to see if he had a signal.

"Who are you going to call?" Morgan asked, moving up behind him, the subtle scent of her perfume carrying on the wind, distracting Jackson more than he wanted to admit.

He'd said he was attracted to her.

That had been an understatement.

Attracted, intrigued, compelled.

All of those things, and that was dangerous territory.

He had a case to solve, and being distracted couldn't help. Wouldn't help.

"A friend in New York. I'm going to have him find Sean Macmillan's family. I want to speak with them," he responded, tucking the phone back into his pocket. He'd call after he finished talking to Morgan.

"The Macmillans wouldn't speak to the media during the trial," she recalled. "I don't think they spoke to anyone. I approached them the first day, wanting to offer my sympathy, but they wouldn't acknowledge me. I always wondered if they believed the lies and thought I was responsible for his death."

"It's possible they were just grief stricken and trying to cope the best way they could. Can you give me their names?"

"I wish I could. It's sad that Sean was such a good friend and I never asked who is parents were or where they lived or even if he had siblings."

"Regret is a bitter pill to swallow," Jackson responded, knowing that his own regrets were a hot, biting taste on his tongue.

"You sound like you know what you're talking about."

"Everyone has regrets, Morgan."

"But yours are about your sister, aren't they? You think you could have saved her. That somehow you're responsible for her death."

Surprised, he turned to face Morgan. Rain had soaked her hair, plastering it in a dark, shiny cap against her scalp. Mud-splattered clothes hanging like wet rags from her frame, she still managed to look confident, strong and beautiful.

"I'm not going to lie and say you're wrong," he responded.

"But you're not going to admit I'm right?"

"Something like that."

"It wasn't your fault, what happened to your sister."

"No. It wasn't."

"But?" she asked, shivering as a gust of wind whipped the drooping edges of her jacket.

"You're freezing. Let's go inside. We can talk more in the morning." He put an arm around her shoulders, urged her toward the house.

"But we won't. Not about your sister, anyway."

"No amount of talking can change what happened."

They reached the door, and she stopped, looked up into his face. "It really wasn't your fault, Jackson. I hope you know that."

He wasn't sure he did. As a matter of fact, he wasn't sure he knew anything. Not at that moment, not with Morgan standing so close, her pale eyes shining with compassion and sorrow, her lips soft and wet with rain.

He leaned down, tasted the icy water on her lips, heard her gasp, felt her press closer.

The door swung open, and Morgan jumped back, her hand to her lips, her eyes wide with shock as Helen appeared in the doorway.

"I was just coming to get you. I've made some tea. I thought you could both use some warming up."

"Actually, I think I'm going to take a hot shower and go to bed, Aunt Helen. I promised Lauren I'd make it to church, and I don't want to look like a walking zombie when I get there."

"I can bring a cup to your room and set it on the bedside table. How does that sound?" Helen offered, and Morgan nodded.

"That sounds good. Thanks." She hurried away, and Jackson had the distinct impression that a hot shower and a cup of tea were the last things on her mind. As a matter of fact, she looked more like a woman with a plan than one with sleep on her mind.

Maybe she thought doing more research, finding more answers, would hasten Jackson's departure from her life. Or maybe she simply thought keeping busy would help her forget the kiss they'd shared.

"How about you? Tea?" Helen asked.

"Sure." He'd take the tea, make a phone call and then go make sure that Morgan was in her room. No way did he want her sitting on the porch swing again.

Helen handed him a heavy mug, steam still rising from it. "I noticed you didn't have a suitcase with you."

"I was trying to keep up with your niece and didn't have time to pack."

"I bet not. Morgan has never been one to sit still and wait for life to happen to her. I'm sure once she made the decision to come back to Washington, she jumped headfirst into the plan."

"She did. We had a wedding to attend this morning, and she had her bag packed and was ready to drive to the airport as soon as it was over. Didn't leave me any time to get my things together."

"I thought you'd just met."

"We did."

"But you were both at the same wedding?" Helen asked, her suspicion obvious.

"Mutual friends. That's why I was in Lakeview. I'm actually from New York," he explained, not bothered by her questions, just anxious to answer them and move on. Time was ticking, and he didn't want to waste any more of it.

"I guess it was a fortunate meeting then, since you saved her life. Listen, I've got some…things you might be able to use."

"Things?"

"Some men's clothes. They're seventeen years past their expiration date, but I guess jeans and T-shirts never go out of style. That's all my husband ever wore."

Husband? Helen had been married? Seventeen years, she'd

said. That was a long time to keep someone's clothes. "I appreciate the offer, but my clothes will dry soon enough. No need to lend me something that's obviously important to you."

"They're just clothes, Jackson, and if I hadn't wanted you to borrow them, I wouldn't have offered. You're about the same size as Darren was. No sense in you sitting around in wet things." She said it matter-of-factly, and Jackson wondered if he'd been wrong to think she'd clung to her husband's clothes and to his memories during the past seventeen years.

"In that case, I'll take you up on your offer."

"I'll leave some things in the hall bathroom. I'm going to bring Morgan her tea, and then I'm going to take a cue from her and go to bed. Good night."

"Good night." Jackson waited for her to disappear down the hall, and then pulled out his cell phone for the second time, glancing at the clock as he dialed Kane's number.

The phone rang twice before Kane answered. "Getting an early start on your day, Sharo?"

"We had some uninvited visitors."

"Everyone okay?"

"For now."

"So, what do you need from me?"

"I'm looking for the parents of Sean Macmillan. I'd find them myself, but I've got a few other people to track down, and we're running out of time."

"The guy killed by his business partner a while back?" Kane asked, and Jackson was sure he heard the rapid tap of fingers on a keyboard.

"That's right. Cody Bradshaw murdered the guy in cold blood."

"That's not what the newspapers said."

"It's what his ex-wife said."

"And you believe her?"

"The other choice is to believe a murderer and his parents, so, yes."

"What do you need me to do?"

"Just find the Macmillans' contact information, see if you can get them on the phone. I'd like to know about anything unusual that happened to their son during the months before he died."

"You think they'll have that information? Seems to me, he was a grown man and probably didn't tell his family much."

"I'm hoping they've got something because right now we're coming up empty. No leads. No ideas. Just a blank slate to build the investigation on."

"Isn't that the place we always start?"

"Yeah, but I usually don't have a woman's life in my hands."

"I'll see if I can find them. If I do, I'll call you with the information."

"Thanks, Kane."

"Just watch your back. I don't want to lose an investigator. Finding someone else is too much of a pain."

"Thanks for your overwhelming concern."

"Thank me after you get back here in one piece." Kane hung up and Jackson did the same, knowing he could count on Kane to find Sean's parents and get whatever information there was.

Which left him to tackle the Bradshaws. Morgan had said that they'd taken possession of Cody's things after he'd gone to prison. Maybe, somewhere in the mix of what they knew and what they had, he'd find something that would lead him to the disk and to whoever it was that wanted it.

He hoped it would, but he wasn't counting on it.

He walked down the hall and into the bathroom, grabbing the clothes Helen had left and changing quickly. Faded jeans. A faded T-shirt. A flannel button-down shirt that looked a lot like the one Helen had been wearing. They weren't his size, but they were close enough and a whole lot better than sitting around in wet clothes.

What had happened to her husband? Had he walked out, died, disappeared?

Jackson wouldn't ask. Whatever had happened seventeen years ago was Helen's business. Jackson's business was keeping Morgan safe.

He walked to her room and knocked on the door, knowing she was awake.

"Yes?"

"It's Jackson."

"I'm sleeping."

"And talking at the same time?"

"People do it all the time," she responded, but the doorknob wiggled and the door swung open. "What's going on? Is everything all right?"

"That's what I was going to ask you."

"I suppose that saying I really was sleeping while I'm standing here in mud-splattered pajamas isn't going to work."

"No."

"Come in for a minute, but keep the door open. Helen's got strict house rules."

"I sensed that about her."

"It doesn't bother me now that I'm an adult, but the first summer I was here, I tried to run away three times. The problem was, getting out onto the main road was a long walk. I was never able to make it before Helen noticed I was gone and came after me." She spoke quickly as if she thought filling each moment with words would keep him from mentioning the kiss.

"Disappointing."

"I pretended it was, but I was always secretly relieved when she showed up. The woods around here can be spooky when you're a thirteen-year-old kid."

"Is that why you finally stopped trying to run?"

"I finally stopped running when Helen put some clay in my

hands and told me to make something." She smiled and walked across the room, her movements nervous and tense. "I decided to call my ex-in-laws."

"I thought we agreed that I'd take care of that."

"We did, but I thought they might be willing to share certain information with me. Information they might not share with the police or anyone else."

"Like?"

"Cody enjoyed having money. It paid for the things he liked. Good food, expensive cars. Beautiful women," she said, confirming what Jackson already suspected.

"He was an idiot."

"So was I, but that's a conversation for another time." She smiled, but it didn't hide the sadness in her eyes. If Cody weren't already dead, Jackson would be tempted to cause the guy some serious pain for what he'd done to Morgan.

"I take it his parents knew about his infidelity?"

"Knew about it or suspected it. Either way, I'm sure they decided it was my fault. I called them, because I was sure that Cody's mother would want to rub it in my face, make sure I suffered as much as her son had. I was right."

"What did she say?"

"Simply that she wasn't surprised to hear from me. That she knew I'd hear about Cody's murder eventually. I offered my sympathy, then asked if he'd been acting okay during the days leading up to his death."

"Had he?"

"She said that he'd been fine, happy even, and that it wasn't just a mother's wishful thinking that made her say that. His girl-friend of five years had thought the same."

"Five years?"

"Whether or not it really was that long, I don't know."

"Did she give you a name?"

"Of course not. She wanted to hurt me. Not help me." She sighed and dropped onto the edge of the bed.

"So, a dead end."

"Not quite. I asked about the disk. Told her that finding it would help the police find the person who killed Cody. Mrs. Bradshaw told me that Cody had them send a box of things to someone a few weeks before he was arrested."

At her words, Jackson's heart leaped. "What was in it?"

"She didn't know. Cody had it packaged and addressed. Apparently, he stopped by their house and asked his mother to overnight it to a female friend of his, someone who lived in the Spokane area. Those were her words, not mine."

"So, he sent something to his girlfriend? The one he'd been with for five years?"

"It looks like it, but who knows? Mrs. Bradshaw is good at making up stories. Maybe that's what she was doing."

"Why would she?"

"To hurt me. For her, there wouldn't have to be any other reason."

"You should have waited for me to make the call, Morgan. Let me handle her," he said, sitting beside her on the edge of the bed, sliding his arm around her shoulder. She stiffened, but didn't pull away.

"I can't keep counting on you to help me, Jackson."

"Why not?" He cupped her jaw with his hand, barely touching the bruised flesh as he urged her to meet his eyes.

"Because…" Her voice trailed off and she shook her head, pulling away and standing up, pacing across the room.

"I'm not your ex-husband, Morgan."

"I know that."

"Then why are you so afraid of what you feel when you're with me?"

"Who said I feel anything?"

"The kiss we shared, for one."

"I was hoping you wouldn't mention that." She turned to face him again, smiling sadly.

"Why? It happened. I'm not sorry it did. I hope you're not either."

"I'm not, but that doesn't mean I want it to happen again."

"No?" He took a step toward her and she raised a hand, stopping him before he could prove her wrong.

"Even if I do, I won't let it. I've been hurt too much, Jackson. I can't be hurt again."

There were a million things Jackson wanted to say in response. A million things he could say, but now wasn't the time. "I can promise you I'll never hurt you, but I don't think you'll believe me. Not now, anyway. So how about I just say good night? We're both exhausted. A few hours of sleep will do us a world of good."

"All right," she said, a weary edge to her voice. She pushed strands of inky-black hair behind her ear, her hands trembling.

"We'll get the answers we need, Morgan, and you'll be able to go back to your life."

"I know. That's not what I'm worried about."

"Then what *are* you worried about?"

"Finding out something I don't want to know. Like who the woman was that Cody sent that package to."

"You don't want to know?"

"I haven't decided yet. It was bad enough knowing my ex-husband was cheating on me. Knowing who he cheated with may just make things worse."

"Is that possible?"

"It is if I know the woman," she said, standing and stretching. "I've got to take that shower and get into bed. The sun will be up soon."

"And you don't want to disappoint Lauren by missing church," he said, letting her change the subject.

"Right. Good night, Jackson."

"Good night," he said, walking out into the hall and closing the door, Morgan's words echoing through his head.

It is if I know the woman.

Was that the reason Cody's mother had been willing to share the information? Was the other woman someone Morgan knew?

One way or another, they had to find out.

Jackson hurried back to the den, ready to make his second early-morning phone call of the day, praying that whatever Sheriff Reed found out, it wouldn't cause Morgan any more pain than she'd already experienced.

SIXTEEN

Three hours of sleep wasn't nearly enough, and as Morgan downed her second cup of coffee and finished eating a slice of buttered toast, she wondered if she should pull off the soft jersey dress she wore, throw back on her pajamas and go back to sleep.

She frowned, setting a crumb-covered plate into the sink and washing her hands. She'd made a promise to Lauren, and she planned to keep it no matter how tired she felt.

How exhausted.

Frustrated.

Angry.

How could it be that after so many years, that even after his death, Cody could still make her feel this way?

So what if he'd sent a package to another woman? It *didn't* matter. So why had she spent most of the hours before dawn trying to put a face and a name to the package's recipient?

And why was she thinking about it now?

Frustrated, Morgan grabbed her purse, scrounged through the bookshelves in the living room until she found a Bible and started for the door.

"Going somewhere?" Jackson's voice was so unexpected, Morgan jumped, her pulse leaping, her stomach churning with the kind of anticipation she had no right to feel. If she could have ignored him and gotten away with it, she might have done just that.

Coward.

The word whispered through her mind as she turned, her breath catching as she met his eyes. She'd expected him to be sleeping soundly, but should have known better. If she'd learned anything about him during the past two days, it was that Jackson was dogged in his pursuit of a goal. And his goal was to keep her safe.

She still wasn't sure how she felt about that.

"I told you I was going to church this morning."

"Maybe I should rephrase the question. Are you going somewhere *without me?*"

"We all had a late night. I didn't want to wake you or Helen." At least that was the excuse she'd given herself when she'd decided to get ready and go to church alone.

The truth was a little harder to swallow.

Jackson was getting under her skin and settling in. Putting some distance between them for a few hours seemed like a good idea.

He raised an eyebrow, but didn't comment. Obviously, he'd been up and getting ready for a while. He was dressed as he had been the previous day. Dark slacks. White dress shirt. Black loafers. All of it clean and pressed. Apparently, he'd found and made use of Helen's laundry room. A tie hung loose around his neck and he'd managed to find a razor and had shaved the auburn stubble from his face. He looked good. Too good, and Morgan turned away. "I made coffee. You want a cup before we go?"

"That and some breakfast. Does your aunt keep the fridge stocked?"

"It's slim pickings but there's bread and eggs and milk."

"Good enough. When do we need to leave?"

"Five minutes ago."

"Then I guess I'd better hurry. Want to come in the kitchen? I've got some information that I want to go over with you."

"Information?" Her stomach churned again, but for a different reason. As much as she wanted answers, as much as she wanted to face the past so that she could put it behind her, she didn't really want to know who Cody had been having an affair with.

"Sheriff Reed spoke with the Bradshaws."

"Did he?"

"He asked them about the package, but they denied any knowledge of it. Said you were lying."

"That figures."

"He didn't push them. He figured there were other ways to get the information." He poured a cup of coffee as he spoke, grabbing bread and dropping two slices into the toaster, moving as if he were as comfortable there as he was in his own place.

Maybe he was.

Maybe Jackson was that kind of person. The kind who fit in wherever he went, who easily made himself at home no matter where he was. The kind of person Morgan had often wished she could be.

"Are you going to keep me in suspense or tell me what he found out?"

"He told them he needed a list of Cody's clients, and they sent an electronic file of his e-mail address book. Sheriff Reed sent it to me. He wants you to look it over and see if there's anyone on it you know."

"That could be hundreds of people."

"It was. I've already narrowed it down," he responded, topping off his coffee and liberally buttering both slices of toast.

"How?"

"I called in a few favors, had some investigators I work with help me do Internet searches on the names. We were able to pare the list down to seven people who live in Spokane and the surrounding areas."

"You must have been up all night."

"Most of it, but the results were worth the missed sleep." He pulled a folded piece of paper from his pocket, held it out.

Morgan took it, her heart beating a strange, sick rhythm. She knew the truth about her ex, but on most days, she preferred not to think about it.

Her hands trembled as she unfolded the paper, and she wondered if Jackson noticed.

It didn't matter.

All that mattered was reading the list of names. Getting the answers they needed.

She scanned the list, looking at names, but not really seeing them.

"Do you recognize any of the names?"

She blinked, trying to bring the paper into focus. "Luke Sanders. He owns a golf resort on Newman Lake. We vacationed there a couple of times after we moved to New York."

"Was he a client of Cody's?"

"I think so."

"Anyone else?"

"Daniel Wilfred was a friend of Cody's during college. I think he's a doctor in the area. Probably also a client of Cody's. Shannon Mallory was an old friend of mine from college." And she couldn't think of any reason why Cody would have been e-mailing her. She didn't say that. She didn't have to.

Jackson frowned, placing his empty toast plate into the sink. "I don't suppose Cody was planning a party for you? Birthday? Anniversary? Is it possible that he was contacting her via e-mail, trying to surprise you?"

"Too much effort. He believed in quick, easy things. Jewelry. Spa days. Theater tickets. A party wasn't something he would ever have planned."

"So, maybe we need to speak to Shannon. Find out why Cody was e-mailing her."

"I guess so."

"Do you have her contact information?"

"Yes." She'd called Shannon a couple of weeks after she'd walked out on Cody and had left a message on her machine. She'd never gotten a response. That hadn't surprised Morgan. She and Shannon had lost touch and reconnected several times since college. Now she wondered if there was more than a busy schedule responsible for the unreturned call. "I've got a phone number and an address. And, now, her e-mail address. I shouldn't have any trouble getting in touch with her."

"How about we tackle that after church? Fifteen minutes ago you said we should have left five minutes ago. Which makes us twenty minutes late."

A reprieve, and Morgan was glad about it.

She and Shannon had shared a dorm room for four years, and when Morgan married it had seemed natural to ask her to be a bridesmaid. A year later, Shannon had gotten married and Morgan had been a bridesmaid at *her* wedding. When Shannon divorced, she'd spent two weeks with Morgan and Cody, getting her thoughts together, mourning the end of something she'd thought would last forever.

Was that all she'd done?

Morgan didn't want to think about the possibility, didn't want to imagine that her good friend and her husband had an affair. Didn't want to, but couldn't seem to stop the thought from circling through her head.

Shannon and Cody.

Cody and Shannon.

Was it possible?

When Morgan thought back, when she tried to pinpoint the moment when her friendship with Shannon had changed, that would be it. After those two weeks, Shannon had been more distant and much more difficult to reach. Morgan had chalked it up to grief, had convinced herself that Shannon was just trying to put the past behind her.

She'd been burying her head in the sand, refusing to see what was right in front of her.

Would acknowledging it have changed the way things had played out? Would it have somehow led Morgan and Cody down different paths? Kept Sean alive? Prevented the nightmare that had been playing out over the past several days?

Morgan walked outside and took a deep breath of cold, crisp air. There were no answers to her questions. No way of knowing what might have been.

The rain had stopped and watery sunlight filtered through the trees. Birds sang. Leaves rustled. All was right with the world.

And everything was completely wrong.

Morgan knew the pain of betrayal. She'd felt it when she was a kid abandoned by her mother and again when she'd realized that Cody wasn't faithful. She hadn't ever wanted to feel it again.

Too bad she didn't have any say in it.

"Ready?" Jackson opened the car door and Morgan climbed in, unable to speak past the lump in her throat.

She'd call Shannon after church.

Or maybe she should call now.

After all, what was the sense in putting it off?

She pulled out her cell phone as Jackson got into the driver's seat.

"Where are we heading?" he asked, and she quickly typed the church name and road into the GPS system.

"That should do it." Her voice sounded raspy and old, and she swallowed hard, trying to clear her throat. "I'm going to call Shannon now."

"It can wait."

"It can't, and we both know it. Besides, putting it off won't change anything. If she and Cody were having an affair, it's water under the bridge. Right now, all I care about is finding that disk." That was partially the truth, and she clung to it as she dialed the familiar number.

One ring. Two. Maybe Shannon had gone to church, though Morgan had never known her to be the kind to attend regularly. Three rings. Four. Morgan expected the answering machine to pick up, and she took another deep breath, preparing to leave a message.

"Hello?" Shannon's voice was such a surprise, Morgan's voice caught in her throat and she couldn't respond.

"Hello? Is someone there? If this is a crank call—"

"It's me, Shannon. Morgan."

There was a heartbeat of silence, and Morgan wondered if Shannon would hang up.

"Morgan…what a surprise. It's been a while."

"A few years."

"I guess you went back to your maiden name. It's on the caller ID and I didn't recognize it." Which was probably the only reason why she'd picked up.

"I thought it would be easier to use my maiden name. Too much publicity around Cody's."

"I'm sure it's been tough."

"It has been, but I wasn't calling to discuss my relationship with Cody."

"No?"

"I'm in town. Staying with my aunt. I was hoping I could stop by and see you."

"I'm really busy right now, Morgan. Work has been crazy, and I—"

"Cody sent you a package before he went to prison."

"I don't know what you're talking about."

"Of course you do. Cody's mother mailed it out for him."

"It's not what you think."

"Yes it is, but that's not what I care about. I need to know what was in the box, Shannon."

"I can't tell you that."

"Why not?"

"Cody gave it to me in confidence, and I promised I wouldn't tell anyone about it."

"Don't you think the fact that he's dead relieves you of the obligation to keep that promise?"

"He's dead?"

"You didn't know?"

"That can't be. I spoke to him..."

"When?"

"Last Sunday. Right before I left on a business trip."

"He was killed five days ago. Didn't his parents tell you?"

The silence on the other end of the line was deafening, and Morgan's hand tightened on the phone. "Shannon? Are you still there?"

"I'm here. His mom left two messages, but she didn't say why she needed to speak to me, and I've been too busy to call her back." Her voice sounded tinny and small, as if the news had stolen something from her. Maybe it had. Unlike Morgan, Shannon may have never accepted the truth about the man she thought she loved.

"I've got to know what's in the box. It's the only way we can find the person who killed him."

"I've got it here, and you're welcome to it. When do you want to come by?"

"Noon?"

"I'll be here." She hung up, and Morgan did the same, her stomach churning, her head pounding. She wanted to tell Jackson to turn the car around and go back to Helen's place, but what good would it do to hide away? She couldn't hide from the truth and couldn't avoid doing what needed to be done. In a few hours, she'd have to face Shannon. Whether she wanted to or not.

And she most definitely did not.

"I'm sorry." Jackson squeezed her hand.

"It's okay."

"It's not, but you will be."

"I know. Shannon says I can come by at noon. She's going to let me have the box."

"And we'll have our answers."

"I hope so. I'm ready to go back to Lakeview and get back to my life."

"You've only been away for a day."

"A day too long. I'm sure you feel the same way about your life."

"Actually, I'm finding this trip a lot more pleasant than I thought it would be."

"You're not going to start that again, are you?" she asked, shooting a look in his direction.

"What?"

"The whole 'attraction' thing."

"It's better than the alternative."

"Which would be what?"

"Letting you sit and mope about your jerk of an ex-husband and his unfortunate love interest."

"I wasn't moping."

"Good, because the jerk wasn't worth it." He grinned, and Morgan found herself smiling in return.

He was right, of course. Cody wasn't worth wasting emotion on. Not regret, not sorrow.

She needed to focus her energy on finding the disk, bringing it to the authorities and making sure that whatever secrets it contained were uncovered. It was the only way to stay alive, and she had plenty to live for. Her family. Her dreams. The brother and sister she wanted so desperately to find.

She shifted in her seat, staring out the window, watching the landscape pass by. Pine trees and mountains, blue sky and white clouds. A simple kind of beauty that she'd missed during her years in New York. She'd said she was anxious to get back to Lakeview, but she wasn't sure that was the truth. What she was really anxious for was resolution and an end to the nightmare it seemed she'd been living for much too long.

SEVENTEEN

If Jackson had had his way when he was growing up, he would have preferred to spend Sunday morning in bed, Sunday night with friends and Wednesday evening playing football. His parents weren't on board with his plans. Sunday morning and evening and Wednesday night were for church activities, and Jackson went whether he wanted to or not.

As an adult, he'd attended church sporadically, often finding it more awkward than comforting. Since Lindsey's death, he'd found himself searching for something that had led him to church over and over again. Faith, maybe. Or hope. Though he didn't often put his longing in those terms. As he pulled into the parking lot of the little country church, he wondered if this would be the place where he'd find what he was looking for.

The thought irritated him. He didn't need to find faith or hope. He'd had it for years. From the time he was a kid, he'd heard the story of salvation and he'd believed it.

So why did he feel so empty?

It was a question he'd been asking himself for a while. One he didn't have an answer to.

"Looks like we're here," Morgan said with a sigh.

"No need to sound so excited about it."

"What's exciting about sitting in church for an hour while everyone stares?"

"It won't be that bad."

"It will if we don't manage to get a seat in the back."

"Don't they always leave that for people who are late?"

"In this church, the back pew is for whoever wants to take a nap while the pastor is speaking."

"You're joking."

"A little," she admitted, pushing open her door and stepping out of the car. "We'd better hurry. Service is about to begin."

Jackson followed her out of the car, walking with her to the church. She was quiet, and he didn't try to engage her in conversation. She was dealing with a lot. Not just the attack against her and the constant danger she was in, but also her husband's betrayal. Her friend's.

He held the door open, and she walked into the church, leading him to a small sanctuary where several dozen families waited for the sermon to begin. Jackson glanced around, searching the faces of the people here, studying each person, trying to find anyone who didn't look like he belonged. Morgan's pursuers would have to be pretty brazen to come inside the church, but that didn't mean they wouldn't do it.

"Let's sit here," Morgan said, tugging Jackson to a back pew and sliding into it, oblivious, it seemed, to his thoughts and his worries.

Jackson dropped down beside her, angling his body so that he could see the entrance to the sanctuary.

"Who are you looking for?" Morgan asked, and Jackson met her eyes.

"Your family." A lie, and Jackson wondered if telling it in church was a bigger sin. Hopefully not. His motivation was pure, after all. Keep Morgan as relaxed and at ease as possible.

Allow her an hour of time when she wasn't worrying about the men who'd chased her from Lakeview.

"Really?" She raised a raven-colored brow, her almond-shaped eyes daring him to continue the charade.

"No."

"You're looking for the men who were at Helen's house last night, right?"

"Not because I think they'll be here, but, yes."

"We weren't followed here. We would have noticed if we had been."

"I wasn't worried about us being followed."

"Then…" She frowned, tucking strands of shiny black hair behind her ear. "You think they followed my family?"

"I don't know, but when it comes to keeping you safe, I want to think of all the possibilities."

"I wish you'd stop saying that."

"What?"

"That you have to keep me safe. You don't. I'm capable of keeping myself safe," she said, but there was no heat in her voice and no fire in her eyes. It was as if she spoke by rote, reciting a well-worn phrase that had no meaning.

"I've got no doubt of that, Morgan, but I've always figured it was easier to face danger with someone than to face it alone."

"The last thing I want is to put other people in danger because of me."

"You're not."

"Then what do you call what happened at my place? You were shot at, Jackson. You could easily have been killed."

"I'm not saying there isn't danger involved in being with you. I'm simply saying that you're not the cause of it."

"Then who is? My dead ex-husband? His girlfriend, or his parents? Some nameless, faceless enemy who wants something I can't give him?"

"Yes."

"Yes?"

"They're all responsible. They all have a part to play in it. You're the innocent bystander in this."

"That's where you're wrong, Jackson. I chose to be with Cody. I chose to marry him despite some niggling doubts about his ability to love anyone beside himself. I chose to stay with him for two years after I first began to suspect he was cheating on me. In that sense, I caused everything that has happened."

"Hindsight is twenty-twenty." He had good reason to know it. He'd spent more time looking back at the year before Lindsey's death than he had looking forward.

"That's the hard thing about life. It's so easy to see what should have been done and said, but so impossible to go back and change it," she said, smiling wanly.

"It's going to be okay, Morgan." He did what he knew he shouldn't and slid his arm around her shoulders, tugging her in closer to his side.

"You keep saying that."

"Because I keep believing that it's true."

"I wish I had your faith."

Faith? Is that what it was?

"Morgan, Jackson! You made it." Lauren's enthusiastic greeting echoed over the sound of quiet conversation, and Morgan shifted, the subtle movement just enough to pull her away from Jackson's arm.

"Did you expect me to do anything else?" she asked as her sister approached, the softness in her voice and face speaking of the love she had for the teen.

"I didn't, but Mom and Dad said you probably wouldn't be here. They said you weren't going to get up early when you didn't have to just because I asked you to." Lauren scooted past Jackson and Morgan and dropped down onto the pew.

"I guess I proved them wrong. Where are they?"

"Coming. They've been stopped in the hall by every single woman here."

"Why's that?" Jackson asked.

"Because Ben is here. He's one of the best-looking single guys to ever grace these halls. Every time he comes for a visit, women swoon."

"That must be making our brother happy," Morgan said with a smile.

"He looks like he's ready to bolt."

"Maybe I should go save him."

"I think staying here is a better idea," Jackson responded, grabbing Morgan's hand when she began to stand. Staying put was better than wandering around. At least here, he had a good view of the entrance and a clear view of everyone in the small room.

He didn't say that, but Morgan seemed to understand. She sank back onto the pew, nodding tightly. "You're right."

"Yeah. Why waste the time and effort? It's not like any of the single women around here are going to stop stalking Ben because you're standing beside him," Lauren said, completely oblivious to the tension. "Look in the front pew, Morgan. See the guy with the dark hair?"

"Yes."

"That's Max. Isn't he cute?"

Jackson couldn't help himself. He looked. There were a couple of teens on the front pew. The dark-haired one was lanky, with shaggy hair and an open, friendly expression. Hopefully it mimicked his personality.

"Yes. Are you two dating?" Morgan replied, and Lauren shook her head.

"Not unless you count going out in a group. Which we're doing this afternoon. The youth group is going to a local convalescent center to sing. You're not going to believe this, but

Max and I are going to sing a duet together. Afterward, the group is going to the mall for some ice cream. If I play my cards right, I might just get to sit next to Max."

Lauren rambled on, and Jackson couldn't help smiling at her enthusiasm. He remembered the days when life had seemed like an endless party. Friends. Dates. The normal adolescent worries.

His cell phone buzzed, and he pulled it from his pocket, glancing at the caller ID and frowning. Kane. If he was calling this soon, there must be news.

"I've got to take this. I'll be back in a minute," he said, interrupting Lauren's monologue.

"Is everything okay?" Morgan asked, the anxiety in her tone obvious.

"I think so. You two stay here, okay? I'll be back in a minute."

She nodded, and he hurried out to the parking lot, dialing Kane's number as he went.

"It's about time," Kane said when he answered.

"What's up?"

"I spoke with Sean's folks."

"Yeah? Get any leads from them?"

"A few things. First, Sean was tense and unhappy the last few weeks before he was murdered."

"Did they know why?"

"They asked, but all he would say was that things at work were hectic and that he had a lot to deal with there."

"That's not much to go on."

"You're right, and I'm confident the police heard the same thing when they interviewed the Macmillans after their son was murdered."

"What else?"

"Seems that Sean wasn't so keen on his business partner's sense of morality. Nor did he think Cody ranked high in integrity. He complained a few times that their business trips often turned into opportunities for Cody to meet up with other women. I guess he wasn't so happy to see his friend cheating on his wife."

"Cody was a real winner. Even his good friend didn't like him."

"Seems that way. From what the Macmillans said, the relationship had been strained for a while before Sean was murdered. Of course, that could just be them twisting the past to match with what they now know to be true."

"It's possible, but I've got a feeling everything they're saying is right on. Do they have any of Sean's things? Work files? E-mail files?"

"It's all in storage, and here's the last point of interest." There was an edge of excitement to Kane's voice that Jackson didn't miss. Whatever was coming was going to be good. "Four weeks ago, someone broke into the storage unit. Went through everything. Even stole Sean's computer system."

Bingo!

"Did they report it to the police?"

"Yes, and they think some forensic evidence was collected at the scene. Maybe a fingerprint, but they're not sure."

"I'll have to call and find out."

"I'm already ahead of you. The Macmillans are in Pennsylvania, and I've put in a call to the local police."

"Thanks."

"No need to thank me. Just make sure you're back and ready to work next week. I've got a full docket of cases, and I need you here ASAP."

"I'll do my best," Jackson responded, saying goodbye quickly and shoving the phone back into his pocket.

It would be interesting to read the transcripts of Cody's trial, see if the prosecution had used the Macmillans as witnesses. They'd obviously had no love for their son's business partner and obviously didn't believe Sean had been murdered because he'd been having an affair with Morgan.

After church, Jackson would make a few calls. See if he could get his hands on the trial transcripts. Right now, though, what he needed to do was get back into church.

He hurried through the quiet hall and stepped into the sanctuary, the sound of a hundred voices lifted in praise filling his ears. His gaze jumped to the pew where he'd left Morgan, and he half expected her to be gone. She wasn't. Sue, Richard and Ben were settled in beside Lauren, standing together pressed shoulder to shoulder, a hymnal held between them. Morgan was to their left near the end of the pew.

She met his eyes as he slid in beside her.

"Who was it?"

"My boss, Kane Dougherty. He's been searching for Sean's parents."

"Did he find them?"

"Yes. They said that Sean and Cody had a strained relationship during the months before their son's death."

"Old news. They brought that up at the trial. It was one of the prosecuting attorney's major themes."

"I figured as much, but they were able to tell Kane something a little more interesting. The storage facility where the Macmillans were keeping Sean's things was broken into a month ago."

"Was anything taken?"

"His computer system. Could be that fits with a standard robbery. Could also be that the system was taken in an effort to find that missing disk."

"Are you two going to whisper sweet nothings into each other's ears all day? Or are you going to sing?" Lauren said loudly enough for the woman in front of her to turn and look.

Jackson chuckled, but Morgan didn't look amused.

"We're not whispering sweet nothings," she hissed in her sister's direction.

"But we could be," he said, leaning close and speaking so softly he knew only she could hear.

She stiffened, her eyes flashing with irritation, but there was something else in her gaze. Fear? Worry?

"You don't have to look so scared, Morgan. I was kidding."

"I keep telling you I'm not scared."

"You shouldn't lie when you're in church."

"And you shouldn't talk when the pastor is getting ready to speak."

"You should both be quiet. Mom and Dad are going to think I'm the one being disruptive, and then I won't be able to go with the youth group this afternoon."

"Sorry," Morgan said, turning her attention back to the hymnal she was holding and dismissing Jackson completely.

That was fine. They'd have plenty of time to discuss why he made her nervous. After church and after they spoke to Morgan's friend Shannon.

Friend?

Not if what Morgan and Jackson suspected was true.

It would be nice if it wasn't. Nice if there was some kind of mistake or misunderstanding, but Jackson wasn't holding out hope for it.

The hymn ended, and he settled down onto the pew, listening as the pastor began to speak. Tired from an almost sleepless night, Jackson wasn't sure he'd be able to keep his eyes open for the sermon, but the pastor was animated and he found himself drawn into the words and the truth they offered. It was a simple message of God's grace. One Jackson had heard a hundred times before. For some reason, this time seemed different. As the pastor spoke of letting go of the past in order to let God into the present, Jackson knew the words were meant for him.

"The past is part of who we are. It formed us and shaped us and brought us to this place, but it does not define us. What defines us now, in this moment, is our relationship with God, our desire to serve Him and our pursuit of His will. We must let go of what was if we are going to embrace what is."

Jackson turned the pastor's words over in his head again and again as the sermon continued.

Let go of what was.

Embrace what is.

What defines us now, in this moment, is our relationship with God.

The truth of the words was something Jackson couldn't deny. He'd avoided church for years, spent a lot of time living life his own way. In the end, that hadn't been enough to fill the emptiness his sister's death had left. It hadn't been enough to ease his guilt or to help him move on with his life.

Maybe the emptiness wasn't just the spot left by Lindsey's death. Maybe it was the emptiness of living a life for nothing but self.

The pastor finished speaking and asked the congregation to rise for the benediction. As he prayed, Jackson prayed, too. For forgiveness. For peace. For the kind of relationship with God that he'd never wanted, but that he was beginning to think he needed.

EIGHTEEN

Morgan moved by rote as the congregation filed out into the aisles. The pastor's sermon had hit home, and she knew she'd have to spend some time thinking about it. Not now, though. Not today. Letting go of the past had ceased to be a possibility two nights ago.

What about having a relationship with God?

The question slipped into her mind and lodged there, filling her thoughts as she stepped out into bright sunshine, Jackson and her family right behind her.

"Are you coming to the house for lunch, dear?" her mother asked, stepping close and taking Morgan's hand. It was the kind of affectionate gesture Morgan had never gotten used to. In Latvia, life had been about survival rather than love, and Morgan had spent the first nine years of her life avoiding the adults who seemed to come and go with abandon.

"I'd like to, but I'm meeting Shannon Mallory at noon."

"Your friend from college?"

"Yes."

"I didn't know the two of you still kept in touch."

"We haven't, but since I was in town, I thought I'd look her up." That was all she would say for now. Sharing the rest with her family wasn't something she felt prepared to do. They probably suspected that Cody hadn't been faithful. Maybe they even knew it for sure, but Morgan didn't want to discuss it with them. She didn't even want to discuss it with Shannon.

"Well, I'm glad you'll be reconnecting with her. You two were so close during college. Maybe if you finish early enough, you can stop by for dinner. I made pot roast for lunch, and I'm sure we'll have plenty left over."

"I—"

"I think that sounds fantastic, Mrs. Alexandria." Jackson spoke up, taking the decision out of Morgan's hands.

That was fine with her. She'd come to Spokane to reconnect with the family, forge the bond that seemed to have always been missing when she was a kid.

"Wonderful! I've still got that huckleberry pie I promised Morgan last night. Dad and Benjamin wanted to eat it for breakfast, but I refused to cut it. The first piece is always for you." She squeezed Morgan's hand, smiling into her eyes, and Morgan's throat tightened with emotion.

"Thanks, Mom."

"For what?"

"Remembering that the first slice of huckleberry pie is always for me."

"You're my daughter. I remember everything about you."

"Hopefully not everything, because there's plenty I'd prefer you forget."

Her mom laughed and released her hand. "We'll see you for dinner."

"You're sure it won't be a problem?"

"Of course. It's actually better this way. Lauren will be home by five. We can all eat together."

"I'll see you then," Morgan said, pressing a kiss to her mother's cheek and doing the same to her father. Then hugging Benjamin and Lauren.

"Ready?" Jackson asked, opening the car door and waiting while Morgan got in.

"I guess I'm going to have to be."

"We could wait."

"For what?"

"For you to be ready."

"How about you just close the door and we get moving? Putting it off is only making me more anxious."

Jackson nodded, closing the door and rounding the car. He seemed distracted as he got in, his gaze on the parking lot and the people who were moving through it.

"What's wrong?"

"Just wondering how long it's going to take for our late-night visitors to return."

"Not long enough."

"That's exactly what I was thinking. Where are we headed?"

"Take I-90 to downtown Spokane. Shannon lives on the south hill."

"Sounds fancy."

"It is. Her ex-husband is a doctor. They bought the house right after they got married. It was part of her divorce settlement."

"How long has she been divorced?"

"Four years," Morgan responded, wiping damp palms on the skirt of her dress. She felt a nervousness way out of proportion to the situation. Whatever had been between Shannon and Cody, it was over. Even if it hadn't been, even if Cody were still alive and the relationship had continued, it shouldn't have mattered. Morgan had walked out on Cody two years ago. She had no claim to him. Wouldn't have wanted one if she'd been offered it.

"What's she like?"

"Shannon? Pretty, fit, fun to be around. Take this exit and turn left when you get to the bottom of the ramp."

"And the two of you got along well?"

"For a while. We had similar interests in college. Art, pottery, sculpting and parties. After college, things changed. We both got married. Lived different kinds of lives, but we were still friends until her divorce."

"And then?"

"We lost touch."

"Just like that?"

"No. She came to stay with Cody and me after her divorce. She said she needed some time away from Spokane and her family. We were happy to have her."

"And now you wish you hadn't?"

Did she? Morgan's marriage had been troubled before Shannon's visit. They'd managed to put on a good show, pretend to be a united front, but reality was that they'd been living separate lives. Cody pursuing his business and Morgan pursuing their marriage. "Nothing would have changed what happened between me and Cody, so even if I could go back in time and uninvite Shannon, it wouldn't make any difference."

"I was thinking about that during the sermon."

"Thinking about what?"

"The past and how easy it is to get caught up wishing we could change it. I've spent two years thinking that I could have prevented my sister's death. If I'd asked the right questions, pushed for answers, maybe she'd still be alive." He shrugged.

"Do you really think you could have saved her?"

"I've spent a lot of time since her death telling myself that I could have. But when I was listening to the sermon today, I started wondering if that was the truth. Maybe I could have changed things with the right question. Maybe I couldn't have, but I can't spend any more time wondering about it. Wishing for it."

"I'm sorry, Jackson." The words weren't enough. Morgan

knew it, but there was nothing else to give, and she put her hand on his shoulder, wishing she could offer more.

"Me, too, but it's time to move on. Time to really put the past behind me. Maybe it's time for you to do the same."

"I wish it were that easy."

"Why can't it be?"

"Because the past is following me, Jackson. Once this is over, once we've got the disk and the police have figured out why someone wants it so badly, then I can move on."

"But will you?"

"Of course. It's what I've been trying to do for years."

"Then why open a pottery gallery in Lakeview, Virginia, when your family is here? This is a beautiful place. I'm sure that for an artist it's full of inspiration."

It was true. She couldn't deny it. "Turn right here. Shannon's house is the cream-colored Victorian on the corner."

"I guess you're not going to answer the question."

"I would if I had an answer," she responded, tensing as he pulled into the driveway of the beautiful old house.

"Think she stuck around and waited?"

"She'll be here. Shannon was never one to back down from a challenge." Morgan took a deep breath and got out of the car, knowing her college roommate was probably staring out a window, watching them approach.

"Come on, then. I'm sure you're as anxious to get this over with as she probably is," Jackson said, taking her hand, tugging her along when she might have been tempted to take another minute, and try to prepare a little more.

"It's an awkward situation."

"Awkward?" Jackson raised a brow, his blue eyes as clear and bright as the summer sky.

"Uncomfortable. Disturbing. Weird. But I figured I'd just go with *awkward*."

Jackson knocked on the door, and Morgan took another deep breath, wiped her palm on her skirt again.

"It's going to be okay." Jackson squeezed her hand, holding it tight as he knocked again.

The door swung open and Shannon appeared, dressed in dark, low-slung jeans and a fitted sweater. Blond hair perfectly highlighted. Green eyes perfectly made-up. Beautiful, but faded since the last time Morgan had seen her. Fine lines fanned out from the corner of her eyes, and her skin seemed a shade too pale.

"Morgan, come on in," she said, stepping aside so that Morgan and Jackson could walk into the large foyer.

"I appreciate you letting me come by to see the box."

"I didn't realize you were bringing someone." Shannon cast a quick glance in Jackson's direction.

"This is Jackson Sharo. He's…a friend."

"I see."

"See what?"

"I guess you really did move on once you left Cody. I'd been worried…" Her voice trailed off and her cheeks flushed.

"That I'd be brokenhearted when I found out you were having an affair with my husband." There. It was out in the open where it needed to be.

"I'm not going to deny it, and I'm not going to apologize. But I will say that I'm sorry to lose your friendship. You always meant the world to me."

Jackson snorted, and Morgan shot a hard look in his direction.

"Sorry, but I don't see how a person could betray someone who means the world to her."

"Let's not make this any more difficult than it has to be," Morgan said.

"It's okay. He's right, but I'm not going to offer excuses. I didn't want to hear them when my husband cheated on me, and I'm sure you don't want to hear them now. You came for the package." She lifted a small box from a round foyer table. "Here you are. There wasn't much in it. Just a personal letter, the necklace I'm wearing and a computer disk."

Morgan tried to avoid looking at Shannon's necklace as she accepted the box, but it was impossible to keep her eyes off it. Large to the point of gaudiness, the heart pendant appeared to be made of diamonds and rubies and looked exactly like one that Cody had given to Morgan six months before she'd walked out on him.

What would Shannon say if she knew that the necklace she wore, the gift she so obviously treasured, was one of two that Cody had purchased?

For a moment, Morgan was tempted to tell her. Tempted to make Shannon suffer just a little of what she had.

She didn't. Wouldn't.

"Have you looked at the disk? Tried to find out what's on it?" Jackson asked, taking a step closer to Morgan, offering silent and unmistakable support.

"No. In the letter, Cody told me not to. He said the information on it could be dangerous."

"Then why pass it on to you?"

"Security. That's what he told me."

"And you were never tempted to take a peek? See what kind of security he was talking about?" Jackson persisted, and Shannon shook her head.

"Why would I be? Cody said the information was dangerous, and I figured the less I knew about it the better."

Morgan took the box from Shannon's hand, doing her best not to notice the tears in her former friend's eyes. She couldn't comfort her. Couldn't offer condolences. Not when the man Shannon mourned was the one she'd betrayed Morgan with. The one who'd betrayed Morgan over and over again.

"I appreciate you letting us have this, Shannon."

"I'm happy to get it out of my hands. Cody said it was his security system. I guess it didn't work nearly as well as he thought it would."

"I guess not. We'd better get out of here and let you get on with your day."

"Morgan..." Shannon's voice trailed off and she shook her head. "Good luck."

"Thanks." Morgan stepped outside, handing Jackson the box and forcing a smile as she offered Shannon a quick wave. "It was nice seeing you again."

The lie rolled off her tongue with relative ease, and she breathed a sigh of relief.

It was over. She'd gotten what she'd come for. Learned what she hadn't wanted to. And it hadn't hurt nearly as much as she'd expected.

"You, too. Take care," Shannon said, shutting the door with a quiet thud.

"I'm impressed," Jackson said as he opened the car door and waited for Morgan to get in.

"With what?"

"The way you handled that. It was a tough situation, but you managed it with grace."

"Only because I was nearly mute with disgust. That pendant she was wearing, the one I kept expecting her to press close to her heart?"

"What about it?"

"Cody gave me one just like it a few years ago. It was a Christmas gift."

"Nice."

"Yeah. Fortunately, I'd already been through a lot with him, and the pendant didn't do anything to convince me that he'd changed."

"I don't think Shannon was nearly as pragmatic about it

as you were. She seemed to think it was a symbol of his undying devotion."

"Maybe because she still believed she was Cody's one true love."

"Cody was—"

"Let's not talk about him, okay?"

"What would you rather discuss?" he asked, pulling out of Shannon's driveway and heading back through downtown Spokane.

"This." She lifted the box with the disk in it. "We need to call Jake and let him know we've got it."

"Right after we make a copy of it."

"Can we do that?"

"Sure. We'll just take it to your parents' place, copy it onto one of their computer hard drives and be done with it."

"That's not what I meant."

"No?" he asked, briefly meeting her eyes before turning his attention back to the road.

"You know it's not. Won't we be tampering with evidence or withholding it or doing *something* illegal with it if we make a copy?"

"Tampering would mean changing it, withholding would mean keeping it from the police. We're not doing either. We're simply waiting a few extra minutes to let the police know what we've got."

"Why?"

"Partially because I'm curious. I want to know what's on that disk, but mostly because I've got a lot of resources at my disposal. The P.I. agency I work for is top-notch, and we've got a computer expert who may be able to track down any leads we find on the disk more quickly than the local P.D. can."

"The police here are first rate. So are the ones in Lakeview," she said, not really protesting Jackson's plan.

"And in New York," he added. "There's no question about that. But once they get this disk, we lose access and control. Personally, I'm not keen on doing either."

Neither was Morgan.

"All right. I like your plan." She typed her parents' address into the GPS system, leaned her head against the seat. Tired. Anxious. They'd be at her parents' house soon. They'd copy the disk, call the police. Would that be the end of the nightmare?

Morgan hoped so.

She prayed so.

But she wasn't sure.

The pastor had said that moving on meant letting go. Jackson had said the same. But how did you let go of something that was part of you? How did you leave something behind when it was constantly there?

It was impossible, of course.

So maybe the point wasn't to forget, but to acknowledge, to learn and then to move forward.

She sighed, closing her eyes. She was too tired for deep thoughts and philosophizing.

Her cell phone rang, and she glanced at the number. Saw that it was her sister. "Hello?"

"Morgan?" Just her name. Nothing more, but there was something in the tone, a trembling, airless quality that had Morgan sitting up straight, her heart pounding rapidly.

"I'm here. Are you okay?"

"You have to do what they say. If you don't they're going to kill me. They have guns. I saw them. Don't call the police. One of them is watching you. He's on I-90. Right behind you."

"Who?" But she knew who, and she reached blindly for Jackson's arm, holding on to the solid warmth of his presence as she shifted in her seat, trying to spot one car in the dozens that were speeding along the highway.

"I don't know. You have something they want. They'll call you later to tell you where to bring it. If you don't—" The word was cut off, the line went dead.

"Lauren? Laur!" Morgan shouted into the phone, knowing her sister couldn't hear, her hand trembling so hard she couldn't hit the button to end the call.

"What is it?" Jackson's question pulled her from the edge of panic.

"They have Lauren." Her voice sounded raspy and hard, her pulse pounding in her ears, filling her throat so that she couldn't breathe.

Jackson swerved to the side of the road, stopping in the breakdown lane and resting a hand against her cheek, staring into her eyes. "Take a deep breath, Morgan."

"I can't."

"Your sister is in trouble. She needs you thinking clearly, not passed out from fear," he said, his voice as hard and unyielding as his hand was warm and gentle.

He was right. Panicking wouldn't change anything. She needed to think clearly. Come up with a plan.

She took a deep breath. Then another. "I'm okay now."

"No, you're not. Neither am I, but we'll have our breakdown *after* we find your sister," he said grimly, his hand dropping away.

"How are we going to do that?"

"I don't know, but the first step is calling the police."

"Lauren said if we do, she's going to be killed. She also said there was someone following us. She even mentioned I-90."

"Yeah?" Jackson glanced into the rearview mirror and pulled back onto the road. "Let's see if we spot a stranded motorist up ahead."

"If we do?"

"We're going to stop and have a chat with him."

Morgan nodded, her throat too tight to speak, her eyes scanning the line of cars ahead of them and the one behind.

Please, Lord, keep Lauren safe. Please, help us find her before it's too late.

Please.

The prayer whispered from the deepest part of her soul, and Morgan let it fly. Hoping God heard. *Knowing* He did.

But would He answer?

That was the struggle. Not with having faith that God *could* step in and help, but with believing that He *would*.

This time, though, she *had* to believe.

If she didn't, if she allowed herself to think that Lauren might die a brutal and horrifying death, she'd melt into a puddle of panic and become completely useless.

"We're going to find her," Jackson said, laying his hand on Morgan's knee, offering a connection she needed more desperately than she ever would have believed she could.

And she covered his hand with hers, linking fingers rather than pushing him away. Clinging to what he offered, praying and hoping it would all be enough.

NINETEEN

Midnight.

Morgan paced the bedroom at her aunt's house, the cell phone clutched in her hand just as it had been for most of the day. There had been no second call. No reassuring sound of her sister's voice. Morgan didn't dare think about what that meant.

The mumble of hushed conversation carried through the closed bedroom door. The family was out there. Mom, Dad, Benjamin, Aunt Helen. Jackson. She didn't need to walk into the living room to know what they were doing. Nursing cups of hot coffee, pacing and praying. Benjamin and Jackson bent over Aunt Helen's computer, searching through the files copied from the disk. Searching for a clue that would lead them to Lauren.

Morgan had stood with them for hours, scanning file after file until her eyes crossed and her head spun. And then she'd walked away, into her room to rest. That's what she'd told everyone.

But she couldn't rest.

All she could do was pace and pray and pace some more.

Not that it was doing any good.

Nearly ten hours had passed since the first phone call. Despite the warning against it, Jackson had insisted on calling the police. Then, just as he'd said he would, he'd copied the disk and handed it over to them with the agreement that it would be kept secret until Lauren was found. To that end, no information was being released to the public. Police channels were silent regarding the case. As far as the world knew, Lauren hadn't been abducted.

If only that were the reality.

Had the men who'd abducted Lauren found out that the police had been contacted? Had Lauren been killed because of what they'd done?

The thought made Morgan sick with fear.

A soft knock sounded on the door, pulling her from her worries.

She thought about ignoring it, pretending that she was asleep so that she could avoid looking into the eyes of the person standing on the other side of the door. Her mother maybe. Or her father. Coming to see if she was all right. Aunt Helen, coming to suggest for the hundredth time that Morgan have something to eat. Or Benjamin, coming to tell her none of what had happened was her fault.

But it was.

For making stupid choices. For sticking with them when she should have walked away.

The knock sounded again, the doorknob turned and the door creaked open.

And Morgan knew it wasn't her parents, her aunt or her brother.

Only Jackson would ignore the closed door and the silence. Only he would be willing to walk in when she'd made it clear she wanted to be alone.

And of all the people in the house, he was the only one she could imagine talking to, sharing her worries with.

"Holding the phone won't make it ring," he said quietly.

"I know."

"And avoiding your family won't make you feel any less guilty."

"I know that, too."

"So, I guess you also know that there isn't any reason to feel guilty. This isn't your fault."

"My head knows it. My heart isn't convinced."

"Come on." He took her hand and led her to the French doors.

"Where are we going?"

"The perfect spot to think," he responded, walking outside and sitting on the swing, tugging her down beside him.

"The problem is that I don't want to think."

"Then how about we talk?"

"Did my family send you to check on me?"

"I volunteered. Everyone is worried about you."

"Why? I'm not the one being held prisoner. I'm not the one in danger."

"Worrying about you doesn't mean they aren't also distraught about your sister."

"I know."

"So why are you here instead of in there with the people who love you?"

It was a good question, a fair one.

And Morgan wasn't sure of the answer.

"I just needed some time alone."

"I guess I can understand that." He rubbed her back, the gesture familiar and easy, as if they'd known each other for years rather than days.

It felt like they had.

Felt as if Jackson had always been part of her life.

"We're going to find her, Morgan."

"I want to believe that, but they haven't called. They should have by now."

"They're criminals. They're not playing by our rules, so they've got no timeline that we can figure out. They'll call, but only when they're good and ready."

"And in the meantime Lauren is counting on me to give them what they want. She's probably wondering what's taking so long." Morgan stood and walked to the edge of the porch, staring out into the darkness beyond, listening to the sound of nature and her own chaotic thoughts.

"She knows you'll do whatever it takes, and she knows we're going to come for her. She's a tough kid. A survivor."

It was true. Lauren had been placed in the foster care system after a teacher noticed burns on her legs and arms. She'd been six at the time and had come to the Alexandria home the same year. Tough and independent and completely unwilling to be part of the family, she'd fought to maintain distance.

Just like Morgan had.

Somehow, though, Lauren had managed to find her niche, to fit in and to make herself part of the Alexandria clan. Nine years after she joined the family, Lauren was a beautiful, well-adjusted young woman. Funny, sweet but still tough as nails. Still a survivor.

"I just wish they'd call," Morgan said, her voice breaking, tears she didn't want to shed sliding down her cheeks. She wiped them away, but they just kept falling. All her fear and worry spilling out.

Jackson pulled her into his arms, and she went, resting her head against his chest, the tears that wouldn't stop soaking his shirt.

"Shh. It's going to be okay," he said, the words tickling against her hair.

"How?"

He didn't answer, and she leaned back, looking up into his eyes, waiting. Wondering what he was thinking. That Lauren was already dead? That they might never find her?

If he was, did Morgan want to know it?

He lifted his hands, ran them lightly over her cheeks, wiping away the moisture, letting his palms drift to her neck and then her shoulders, leaving a trail of heat and of comfort that Morgan couldn't deny.

She should move away. She knew it, but didn't.

Finally, he spoke, his words filling the silence. "I don't know how it will be okay, but I believe it will be. For now, that's all I've got to offer."

"I'd rather have that than a lie."

"I'll never lie to you, Morgan. Not about this. Not about anything else."

"What else will there be? We'll find Lauren, the men who took her will be punished and then we'll both move on with our lives."

"Is that the way you really want it? This thing plays out and then we go our separate ways?"

She could lie and say yes, or she could give him the same honesty he'd given her.

"I don't know."

"I guess that will have to be enough for now." He smiled, leaning forward and pressing a gentle kiss to her lips.

Surprised, she stepped back. "You shouldn't have done that."

"Maybe not, but I did. I guess I can't take it back. Even if I could, I wouldn't."

"Morgan? Jackson? You guys in there? The police just phoned." Benjamin called into the open door of the bedroom, his voice carrying out onto the porch.

Morgan's heart leaped at his words, and she hurried into the bedroom, Jackson close behind her.

"Have they found her?" Morgan asked, hope soaring and then crashing back down again when she saw her brother's grim expression.

"No, but they found her purse shoved into a trash can in the women's restroom at the mall. House keys. Wallet. Everything was still in it. Even her cell phone. The last call Lauren made from it was to Morgan. The police are looking at security video of the area to see if they can spot her. Maybe get a look at the person who took her. They're not releasing any information to the press, and the case is still being conducted with caution. No information going out to anyone."

"Good. We don't want to scare off the quarry," Jackson said, and Benjamin nodded.

"I couldn't agree more. I'm going out for a while." He turned to leave the room.

"Going where?" Jackson followed, and Morgan could feel the tension pulsing in the air.

"To look for my sister."

"That's not a good idea. It's better to stay here and wait—"

"We've been waiting for hours. I'm done with it. I know Lauren was taken from the mall. I'll start searching there. They couldn't have taken her far."

It wasn't true. They could be hundreds of miles away by now, but Morgan didn't say it. She understood Benjamin's need to go and do rather than to sit and wait, and she put her hand on Jackson's arm.

"It's not going to do any harm for him to look. Let him go."

"It's better if we're all here. At least then, we don't have to worry about someone else being taken."

Benjamin smiled darkly. "Let's hope that's exactly what happens. They get their hands on me, I'll wait until I'm with Lauren and then let them know exactly what kind of mistake they've made."

He stalked from the room and down the hall. Morgan heard a quiet rumble of voices, her mother's higher-pitched protest and then the door opened and closed with sharp finality.

"I'd better go call this in. Are you going to be okay?" Jackson stepped into the hall, hesitating near the threshold of Morgan's room.

"Fine. I'll be out in a minute."

He nodded, disappeared down the hall just as Benjamin had moments ago.

And Morgan was left alone again.

Exactly the way she wanted to be.

But somehow being alone wasn't nearly as comforting as she'd thought it would be. She stepped back out onto the porch, tensing as the sound of a car speeding away filled the air. Benjamin was in a hurry, but that had always been his way. Quick to act. Sometimes just as quick to regret it.

She hoped he wouldn't be this time. Hoped he wasn't putting himself in danger. Maybe putting Lauren in more danger.

If that was even possible.

Her little sister was being held by the same kind of men who'd nearly killed Morgan. Maybe the same men. And there was nothing Morgan could do about it.

Please, Lord, keep her safe. Please, don't let anything happen to her.

The prayer welled up and spilled out, the darkness pressing in, more comforting than frightening, the sounds of the woods and of the night seeming to whisper that God was in control and that everything would be all right.

And Morgan wanted to believe it.

Her cell phone rang, the sound so startling Morgan almost dropped the phone. She fumbled to answer, her heart racing as she lifted it to her ear. "Hello?"

"I guess you decided to be smart for a change." The silky voice froze the blood in Morgan's veins, wiped every thought from her head. She knew the voice. Had heard it a few nights ago.

"What do you mean?" Her voice trembled, and it infuriated her. She wouldn't let this man know how scared she was. Wouldn't let him know how the sound of his voice terrified her.

"We've been watching and listening, making sure you didn't

contact the police. Your sister's life depended on it. I guess you care more about her than you do about yourself, seeing as how you let us beat you senseless the other night. You could have saved us all a lot of trouble if you'd just told us where to find the disk."

"Get to the point. What do you want?"

"Whatever it was you carried out of your friend's house. You bring it to us. We give you your sister. It's as simple as that."

"How do I know she's still alive?"

There was a moment of silence, then Lauren's voice, trembling and raspy. "Morgan? I'm okay. Don't worry about me and don't do what they tell you. They're just—"

Her words were cut off, and Morgan tensed. "Lauren?"

"She's fine, but she won't be if you don't do exactly what we tell you."

"I'm listening."

"You're going to bring us what you've got. You're going to come alone. If we get any hint that you've been followed or that you've called the police, your sister dies. Understand?"

"Yes."

"I've got a friend waiting for you at the end of the dirt road. He says someone just left there in a hurry. I hope whoever it is isn't going to the police."

"He's not."

"Good. So, here's what you're going to do. Run down the road. My friend will meet you partway up it. You've got fifteen minutes to meet him. If you're not there in that time, your sister is going to suffer." The phone clicked, and Morgan shoved it into her pocket.

Fifteen minutes.

It wasn't a lot of time. She needed to leave now.

But first she needed to get the disk.

No. She needed to get *a* disk.

She scrounged through the small desk in the corner of the

room, pulled out a USB device and shoved it into her pocket. No box, but that was okay. Until Lauren's abductors tried to open the files, they'd have no idea whether or not Morgan had brought them what they wanted. That played in her favor. While they searched, she and Lauren could try to escape.

It sounded like a good plan. Even a reasonable one. As long as Morgan didn't think about all the things that could go wrong.

She stepped outside, jumping off the porch and running around the side of the house. The dogs began barking, their furious warning spurring Morgan on. Past the house and the front door that was spilling light onto the porch.

She heard someone call out, but she ignored it, running full speed down the driveway and onto the road. She'd come this way plenty of times when she was a teen, running away from Helen and toward something she craved, but couldn't quite define. She'd never put much effort into it then. Now, she ran as if her life depended on it because Lauren's life did. Fifteen minutes was enough time if Jackson didn't follow. If her parents and Helen didn't. She expected to hear footsteps pounding the pavement behind her. Maybe a car engine springing to life. Expected someone to try to stop her. Half hoped someone would.

She heard nothing but her gasping breath and racing pulse.

Up ahead, headlights flashed as a car sped toward her, braking hard just a few feet away. The door opened as she approached, and icy fear nearly stopped her in her tracks. Only the thought of Lauren, scared and alone, kept her moving. To the car. Into it. Slamming the door shut. Praying that she wasn't making the biggest mistake of her life.

TWENTY

Jackson crouched in the shadows of the trees, frowning as the car maneuvered into a U-turn. He wanted nothing more than to jump up, race forward and yank open Morgan's door, pulling her out and back to safety.

But saving her might mean losing Lauren, and Jackson knew Morgan wouldn't thank him for it. He wouldn't thank himself for it, either. So he waited, anger simmering at a low heat in his gut, his muscles tense with fear and frustration as he noted the details of the car. A Toyota. Two-door. Late model. License plate splattered with mud and only partially visible. XL-something. Turning left at the highway, heading toward Spokane.

He pulled out his cell phone, calling the local police chief and filling him in on the situation, giving him the information and ignoring the man's orders to stay put. No way was he going to do that.

Morgan should have told him she'd gotten the call. Should have given him five minutes to come up with a plan. Instead, she'd jumped headfirst into action. No plan. No discussion. Which left Jackson with no choice but to try to follow along, see if he could keep the situation from escalating.

Behind him, a car approached, tires rolling along the dirt.

Slow and cautious. Lights off. Just the way Jackson had told Morgan's father to come.

He straightened, motioning for Richard to pull forward, then hurried to the driver's side of the car. "Mind if I drive?"

"I don't care who drives as long as we find my daughters." He maneuvered over the gear shift and into the passenger seat, leaning forward and staring out the window. "Did you see them? Did you see Lauren?"

"I'm afraid not, but I did see the car and I know what direction it's headed."

"That's something, I guess."

Jackson pulled out onto the road, flipping on the headlights and picking up speed. The traffic on this part of the freeway was sparse, but up ahead, several cars kept pace with one another. Jackson closed the gap between them. Not hurrying, but not holding back.

At the front of the pack, the quarry was gaining speed. Jackson eased up on the accelerator, not wanting to catch up. All he needed to do was keep the car in his sight. Ten miles. Fifteen. Twenty. The car stayed in front of them, keeping a steady speed. Not doing anything that would get the driver noticed by the police.

"When I get my hands on that daughter of mine, I'm going to give her a piece of my mind. Going off like this. Not letting any of us know what she was up to," Richard muttered, breaking the silence, the worry in his voice obvious.

"Has she always been like this?"

"Impulsive? Yes. She'd make a decision and go off and follow through on it without thinking of the consequences. Got her into a boatload of trouble when she was in high school. Got her married to the jerk. She's matured a lot through that, though. God has a way of helping us grow through the tough times."

"I'm sure knowing that didn't make you any happier to see Morgan marry a guy like Cody."

"No, and it doesn't make me any happier to know she went running from the house rather than coming to us. I just pray that she and Lauren will be okay," Richard replied, leaning forward. "Is that the car? The Toyota?"

"Yes. And it looks like he's going to exit the highway."

"Heading into town. Not the best area to take a ride, though."

"Maybe not, but at least there's traffic moving through it. That makes it easier for us to keep from being spotted." Jackson followed the car through the busy downtown area, hanging back as it turned onto a quieter side street. Boarded-up buildings lined the road, and he expected the car to stop in front of one. Instead, it kept going, up a steep hill and into a neighborhood of 1920s homes.

Jackson put on his blinker and pulled into a driveway, waiting as the car turned onto another street. Then he pulled out again, this time with his headlights off.

The Toyota was several blocks away as Jackson turned, and he followed slowly, hoping the darkness was enough to hide his approach.

The driver turned into the driveway of a run-down house, and Jackson braked, easing the car to the side of the road and cutting the engine. Several minutes passed before the car door opened and a man got out, rounded the car and opened the passenger door.

Jackson tensed, watching as Morgan got out of the car. She didn't fight as she was yanked to the house and shoved inside. Jackson's jaw clenched with anger, and he opened the car door.

"Call the police. Let them know where we are."

" don't think I'm going to sit here waiting while you go
    ughters?"

        eople we've got in danger, the better." He tossed
            ichard's direction and got out of the car.
             if Richard was going to go along with

the plan, just jogged up the street, eased up to the house Morgan had entered.

She was inside with two men who wouldn't hesitate to kill her, and Jackson was outside without a weapon. Somehow, he needed to even the odds. Put himself at the advantage. And he had to do it *before* the police showed up and pushed the two men into action. He crouched low, easing through the dark yard and around to the back of the house, searching for a way in.

An old-fashioned cellar door lay flat against the ground, the hinges rusted. If there was a lock, Jackson couldn't see it. Fear pounded a hollow beat in his throat as he tried to lift the door, finally managed to wrestle it open, wincing as the old hinges creaked in protest.

Stairs led down into the pitch-black cellar, and Jackson moved with caution, lowering the door carefully, not daring to keep it open. Seven steps down, the thick, musty scent of rotting wood and mold filled his nose. Voices carried through the darkness, faint and barely audible. Good. They were still going about their business, unaware that he'd arrived. Across the room, light spilled from a door at the top of rickety steps.

He walked toward it, freezing when something grunted in the blackness to his right. Some*one* grunted.

A woman?

Lauren?

He turned, feeling his way through the inky blackness, nearly falling over someone lying on the floor.

He knelt down, touching soft cloth and cool flesh, running his hand down arms bound with duct tape. "Lauren?"

She grunted, bumping against his questing hand, apparently trying to hurry him along.

"Hold on. I'll untie you." He found the edge of the tape, tore at it for what seemed like an hour but was probably only five minutes. Finally it loosened, and he was able to rip it from her wrists. She gave a muffled yelp.

"Sorry."

Seconds later, he heard the sound of more tape being torn away from flesh. Another quiet yelp. And Lauren's voice, husky and dry. "It took you long enough to get here."

"Sorry, kid. We had a little trouble finding you. Come on, let's get you to your feet and get out of here."

"My ankles are taped, too. The tape is tighter than what was on my mouth. My fingers are too numb to get it off." There was an edge of panic to her voice, and Jackson put a hand on her arm.

"It's okay, Lauren. I'll help."

"But what if they come back? What if…" Footsteps tapped on the ceiling above their heads. "That's them. They're coming. I always hear the footsteps before the door opens."

"Lie down, hands behind your back. Whatever happens, don't let them know you're untied." He hoped she understood. Hoped that she'd do what he said.

There was no time to make sure. Just as she'd said, the door was opening. Jackson slid into the shadows beneath the stairs, waiting. Praying for an opportunity to act. Praying that Lauren wouldn't give him away.

"How about you spend a little time with your sister while we make sure the disk is what we've been looking for?" someone said.

"Whether it is or not, you're still going to end up in jail. No way will you get out of town without being found." Morgan's voice sounded shaky and unsure, and Jackson's muscles tensed. What had happened since she'd gotten in their car? Had she been hurt again?

"If you knew who was backing us, you wouldn't be saying that. He's got money. Plenty of it, and getting us out of town isn't going to be a problem for him."

"Unless he decides he doesn't need you to make it out of town. Maybe he'll just have your buddy bring him the disk and leave you here to rot. Then you'll end up in jail like my ex, while whoever hired you goes on with his life. Give it a year and you'll be dead. Just like Cody."

"Shut up!" A harsh slap followed the command, and Morgan shrieked, the sound echoing through the cellar as she tumbled down the steps, landing in a heap on the floor.

The door slammed, and Jackson lunged forward, scooping Morgan into his arms and knowing it was the worst thing he could do if she had a neck or head injury. "Morgan! Are you okay?"

"I will be once you stop smothering me." Her voice shook, and he could feel her heart pounding frantically. He eased his grip, his hands shaking as he cupped her face in his hands, tried to see through the darkness. Make sure she really was okay.

"I hate to break up the reunion, but I still can't get this tape off my ankles," Lauren whispered, and the fear in her voice spurred Jackson to action. He moved quickly, lifting Morgan and carrying her across the room to her sister.

"Hey, I can walk."

"But you don't have to. Sit here while I get your sister ready to go." It took too long to find the ends of the tape, to unwind the tight bonds from Lauren's ankles. Each minute seemed like an hour, the time ticking in Jackson's head, reminding him that at any moment Lauren and Morgan's captors could return.

Were the police outside, waiting for a chance to bring both men down?

Jackson wasn't going to wait to find out.

He ripped the last piece of tape from Lauren's ankles, patted her foot. "That's it, kid. You're free. Think you can walk?"

"I can't feel my lower legs, but I'll try."

"Jackson can carry you. I can make it out myself," Morgan said, and Jackson could hear her shifting, getting to her feet.

"Works for me." Jackson lifted Lauren's trembling body, was across the room, heading up the steps to the back door when the floor above their heads creaked. He shoved at the heavy door, forced the rusted hinges to move again. Finally, it opened and he set Lauren outside as the other door opened and light spilled into the darkness.

"Hey! What's going on?"

"Look out!" Morgan screamed the warning as Jackson turned, saw the gun aimed at his head. He dove to the side too late. Knew the bullet would find its target.

Morgan moved, leaping into the line of fire, flying backward as the first report exploded through the room.

Somewhere above glass shattered. Men shouted. Another gun exploded, but Jackson's focus was on Morgan, lying in the shadows, blood pooling beneath her, spilling across the dirt-covered floor.

Dead?

Fear and rage filled him, and he ran to her, ignoring the sound of boots pounding above his head, the next sharp report. The clatter and thud as the gunman who'd shot Morgan fell.

Please, God, don't let me lose someone else.

The prayer filled his mind, filled his soul as he ripped off his jacket and pressed it hard against the bleeding wound in Morgan's chest.

TWENTY-ONE

Pain pulled Morgan from silky blackness.

Pain and the sound of someone crying. The quiet rumble of voices. A door closing.

She opened her eyes, groaning as bright light drilled hot pokers into her head.

"Morgan? Can you hear me?" Jackson spoke quietly, his voice pulling her further out of the darkness, and she turned her head. Met his eyes. Felt something inside her shift. Something cold grow warm.

"Is someone crying?"

"Your mother was. Your dad just took her to get some coffee. They'll be back in a minute." His fingers traced a gentle line down her cheek, his palm coming to rest on her shoulder. Light. Warm. Comforting. She wanted to close her eyes again, sink back into unconsciousness.

"Are you planning on leaving again so soon? And here I've been waiting two days to look into those beautiful eyes," he whispered into her ear, his breath tickling her flesh, drawing her back from the edge of darkness.

Two days?

Morgan opened eyes she hadn't even realized she'd closed, blinked, trying to clear her mind.

"I've been here for two days?" Her throat felt hot and sore, and she swallowed hard.

"You went into surgery Sunday night. It's late Tuesday."

"It seemed like just a minute ago...." What? She remembered terror. Remembered Lauren's trembling voice. Jackson's grim one.

Had the unthinkable happened?

Had Lauren died?

"Why was Mom crying? It's not Lauren, is it? She isn't..."

"Lauren is fine. She's got a few bruises, but nothing that won't heal. Your mom was crying because she's been worried sick about you. We all have been."

"I'm okay." She tried to struggle up, but he pressed her back, his touch as light as a butterfly's wing.

"Your clavicle was shattered, and you nearly bled to death. You need to stay still and rest until the doctor tells you differently."

"I'm sorry I worried everyone."

"*Worried* is an understatement. Remind me to lecture you on throwing yourself in front of a bullet once you've recovered." His tone was light, but the concern in his gaze was unmistakable.

"Is that what I did?" The last thing she remembered was tumbling down a flight of steps, hearing Jackson's voice, feeling his arms around her. Hearing Lauren's voice.

Then nothing. Just darkness. And pain.

"You saved my life, Morgan."

"I guess I owed you." Despite her best efforts to keep them open, her eyes closed again. She blinked, tried to focus on Jackson. "What happened? The two men who grabbed Lauren, are they in jail?"

Jackson hesitated, then shook his head. "They're both dead. Killed by the police."

"Then I guess we'll never know who hired them." She

wanted to care, but her body was leaden, her mind fuzzy, the pain that had woken her beginning to fade. Warm contentment taking its place.

"Actually, the police have made an arrest. A circuit court judge in New York City. Edward Santino. He's from a wealthy family. Inherited his father's estate when he was young."

"I've never heard of him."

"You would have eventually. He was being groomed to run for Senate. Probably would have made an appearance in next year's polls."

"What does that have to do with Cody?"

"We think that Santino was on a local drug cartel's payroll, accepting bribes in exchange for lighter sentences. There've been a half dozen drug dealers who walked on technicalities during Santino's time on the bench. The New York State attorney general is investigating, but it looks like Santino has been responsible for a lot of very bad men going free. The disk Cody sent to Shannon listed several offshore accounts where Santino was hiding funds. No proof yet where those funds came from, but there's no doubt the police will find it."

"So Cody decided to blackmail him in the hope that Santino could get him out of prison?"

"Get him out or find a way to shorten his sentence. We're not sure which. Not surprisingly, Santino isn't cooperating with the police."

"With Cody dead, he's probably hoping there won't be enough evidence to convict him," Morgan said, tired, but relieved to have answers. To know at least some of the truth.

To know that Lauren was alive and safe.

That her family was together.

They were good things, and Morgan smiled, her eyes closing again.

She opened them quickly, almost afraid that she'd wake up and find that it was all a dream. That the nightmare wasn't over.

"It's okay. Rest for a while," Jackson said, his lips brushing her cheek.

"I'm afraid to. What if I wake up and I'm back in that cellar in Spokane? Or still in my apartment, blood all over my kitchen floor?"

What if I wake up and you're not here?

She wanted to say it, but the words caught in her throat and she could only stare into his eyes, will him to be there when she woke.

"You won't be. It's over. And when you wake up, you'll still be here in the hospital, and your family will be waiting to chew you out for taking so many risks."

"In that case, maybe being unconscious has some benefits."

Jackson laughed and shook his head. "I'm glad to see that nearly dying hasn't ruined your sense of humor, because there's something else I need to tell you."

"What?"

"I've got a lead on your brother."

"My brother?" She had three and didn't know why he'd need to have a lead on any of them.

Unless he meant Nikolai.

At the thought, Morgan's heart jumped and her muscles tensed. "You mean Nikolai?"

"Yes."

"You've found him?"

"Not yet, but I'm getting close. I found his adoptive family. They live in Florida. Your brother is in the military and they haven't heard from him in two years."

"That's a long time."

"They're as anxious for me to find him as you are."

"You're sure it's him?"

"I'm sure. I traced him from Latvia to an adoptive family in Utah, then into foster care and to the family in Florida."

"He had two adoptive families?"

"The first placement was disrupted. Things didn't work out."

"Poor Nikolai. I wonder if that's why he's disappeared."

"I don't know, but I'll find out. And while I do, I want you to rest and heal. I've got some canoeing to do when I get back to Lakeview, and I want to take you with me when I do it," Jackson said, lifting her hand and pressing a kiss to her knuckles.

"Canoeing?"

"There's nothing more romantic than the lake at sunrise."

"Jackson—"

"It's okay if you're not sure, Morgan. It's okay if you're scared. Your ex was a jerk, and I know you need time and space to heal from that, but I can't turn my back on you. I can't walk away and forget the way I feel when I look into your eyes. I think God brought us together for a reason. I'm willing to take as much time as we need to figure out what that is."

Morgan tensed. Jackson was right. She was scared. To hope. To believe. To trust that what she felt when she was with him was real and right and good.

But moving forward meant letting go of the past. It meant being in the moment, embracing what was, rather than longing for what could have been.

The pastor had said that two days ago, and the words seemed truer now than ever.

She took a deep breath, looking into Jackson's eyes, seeing a future she'd never dared to dream of. "You're right."

"About what?"

"About sunrise on the lake. There's nothing more romantic, and I can't think of anyone I'd rather be there to watch it with than you."

Jackson smiled, leaning down to press a kiss to her lips, the touch as sweet and gentle as the first rays of sun falling across the morning sky, whispering of hope, of love and of the one thing Morgan had always wanted but never quite found—home.

* * * * *

Look for the next book in the
HEROES FOR HIRE *series,*
coming in July 2010!
Only from Love Inspired Suspense.

Dear Reader,

Running for Cover is a story about many things. It is the story of a man who is trying to free himself of guilt, of a woman who is searching for a place to belong and of two people who are clinging to faith as they face an unseen enemy.

While I was writing Morgan and Jackson's story, I was preparing to travel to China to meet my daughter. She'd been through a lot in her seven years of life, and I wondered how someone who had lost so much could ever understand and accept that she is loved by her parents, her siblings and, most importantly, by God. My thoughts about my daughter's life journey are reflected in Morgan's journey from doubt to faith, from loss to love.

I hope you enjoy the first book in the HEROES FOR HIRE miniseries!

I love hearing from readers. If you have time, drop me a line at shirlee@shirleemccoy.com.

Blessings,

Shirlee McCoy

QUESTIONS FOR DISCUSSION

1. Morgan Alexandria moved to Lakeview, Virginia, to escape her past, but running hasn't freed her from the guilt she feels over the mistakes and poor choices she's made. What is it she most regrets about her past, and why does she have difficulty letting it go?

2. Jackson Sharo is also dealing with guilt, but his guilt is of a different kind. Why does he blame himself for his sister's death?

3. Jackson was in the right place at the right time to save Morgan from harm. Do you think this was luck, or did God have a hand in bringing them together? Has anything like this ever happened to you?

4. Why has guilt over his sister's murder led Jackson to quit his job as a homicide detective?

5. Morgan's fresh beginning does not include reconnecting with her adoptive family. Why is it so hard for her to accept the love her family offers?

6. Morgan has no desire to be in a relationship again. She's already failed at marriage, and she doesn't want to risk her heart. What is it about Jackson that makes her reconsider her decision to stay single?

7. Jackson lived a rather wild life before his sister's murder. In what ways has her death changed him? How have those changes prepared him for a relationship with Morgan?

8. Morgan learned to rely on herself at a young age. Having to depend on another person makes her feel weak and vulnerable, and she'd rather go it alone than accept anyone's help. How does this interfere with her relationship with God? How does it keep her from accepting the help Jackson is offering?

9. Jackson promises Morgan he'll help find her biological siblings for her. Do you think Morgan believes he'll help? Do you think she believes she'll find them? Why or why not?

10. During the story, Jackson is searching for redemption. Does he find it?

11. Morgan is searching for something else. What is it that she's hoping to find? What is it that she realizes she needs?

12. Why does personal guilt make it difficult to have a relationship with God? What is God's solution for this?

*When his niece unexpectedly arrives at his
Montana ranch, Jules Parrish has no idea what
to do with her—or with Olivia Rose,
the pretty teacher who brought her.
Will they be able to build a life—
and family—together?*

*Here's a sneak peek of "Montana Rose"
by Cheryl St. John, one of the touching stories
in the new collection,
TO BE A MOTHER,
available April 2010
from Love Inspired Historical.*

Jules Parrish squinted from beneath his hat brim, certain the
waves of heat were playing with his eyes. Two females—one
a woman, the other a child—stood as he approached.

The woman walked toward him. Jules dismounted and approached her. "What are you doing here?"

The woman stopped several feet away. "Mr. Parrish?"

"Yeah, who are you?"

"I'm Olivia Rose. I was an instructor at the Hedward Girls
Academy." She glanced back over her shoulder at the girl who
watched them. "My young charge is Emily Sadler, the daughter
of Meriel Sadler."

She had his attention now. He hadn't heard his sister's name
in years. *Meriel.*

"The academy was forced to close. I thought Emily should
be with family. You're the only family she has, so I brought
her to you."

He took off his hat and raked his fingers through dark, wavy hair. "Lady, I spend every waking hour working horses and cows. I sleep in a one-room cabin. I don't know anything about kids—and especially not girls."

"What do you suggest?"

"I don't know. All I know is, she can't stay here."

*Will Olivia be able to change Jules's mind
and find a home for Emily—and herself?*

*Find out in
TO BE A MOTHER,
the heartwarming anthology from
Cheryl St. John and Ruth Axtell Morren,
available April 2010
only from Love Inspired Historical.*

LARGER-PRINT BOOKS!

**GET 2 FREE
LARGER-PRINT NOVELS
PLUS 2 FREE
MYSTERY GIFTS**

Love Inspired®
SUSPENSE
RIVETING INSPIRATIONAL ROMANCE

Larger-print novels are now available...

LISUSLP10

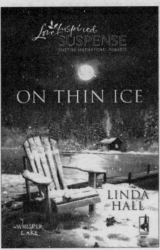

Love Inspired SUSPENSE

TITLES AVAILABLE NEXT MONTH

Available April 13, 2010

ON THIN ICE
Whisper Lake
Linda Hall

DEADLY VOWS
Protecting the Witnesses
Shirlee McCoy

CALCULATED REVENGE
Jill Elizabeth Nelson

MOUNTAIN PERIL
Sandra Robbins

LISCNMBPA0310